ZERO SUM

BOOKS BY JAN THOMPSON

City/Coastal/Beach Romance

Seaside Chapel (7 Books)

JanThompson.com/seaside

Savannah Sweethearts (12 Books)

JanThompson.com/savannah

Vacation Sweethearts (8 Books)

JanThompson.com/vacation

Romantic Suspense/Thrillers

Protector Sweethearts (6 Books)

JanThompson.com/protector

Defender Sweethearts (6 Books)

JanThompson.com/defender

Binary Hackers (4 Books)

JanThompson.com/binary

JanThompson.com/books

ZERO SUM

BINARY HACKERS
BOOK 1

JAN THOMPSON

GEORGIA
PRESS

Zero Sum (Binary Hackers Book 1)

Copyright © 2017 Jan Edttii Lim Thompson
Published by Georgia Press LLC
Author Website: JanThompson.com
Book News: JanThompson.com/newsletter

This book is a work of fiction. Any names, characters, companies, organizations, places, events, locales, and incidents are either used in a fictitious manner or are fictional. Any resemblance to actual persons, living or dead, actual companies or organizations, or actual events is purely coincidental.

Cover Design by Deranged Doctor Design

Scripture taken from the New King James Version®. Copyright © 1982 by Thomas Nelson. Used by permission. All rights reserved.

eBook ISBN 978-1-944188-40-5
Paperback ISBN 978-1-944188-41-2

*To my Lord and Savior, Jesus Christ, who died on
the cross to save me from my sins and rose again
from the grave to give me eternal life in heaven.*

*For God so loved the world that He gave His only
begotten Son, that whoever believes in Him should
not perish but have everlasting life.*
—John 3:16

ABOUT THE BINARY HACKERS SERIES
INSPIRATIONAL ROMANTIC TECHNOTHRILLERS

From *USA Today* bestselling author Jan Thompson come these inspirational near-future cyberthrillers combining technothriller and romance, starting with **Binary Hackers** that feature computer specialists living at the edge of cyberspace, where they have to juggle being law-abiding truth-telling Christians while carrying out their assignments by any and all means possible. If you're looking for clean futuristic romantic suspense thrillers that don't compromise the Christian faith, these books are for you.

The **Binary Hackers** series is set in the same story world as Jan's other contemporary books, and characters from the other series may make cameo appearances in this series and vice versa.

- Book 1: *Zero Sum*
- Book 2: *Zero Day*
- Book 3: *Zero Base*
- Book 4: *Zero Trust*

Binary Hackers
JanThompson.com/binary

Subscribe to Jan Thompson's mailing list:
JanThompson.com/newsletter

ABOUT ZERO SUM
BINARY HACKERS BOOK 1

A broken hacker.
A brave FBI agent.
A deadly brain implant.

In *Zero Sum* (Binary Hackers Book 1), FBI Cybercrime Special Agent Stella Evans finds the last surviving computer consultant who holds the key to destroying a terrorist organization's global network, but Cayson Yang may not live long enough to dismantle the computer system.

The Chaos...

Computer network specialist Cayson Yang's struggling network infrastructure company has received a rash of new clients lately, the total income of which finally puts Binary Systems, Inc., in the black for the first time ever. He is now able to give pay raises to himself and his business partner and cousin, Leland Yang-Joule, and bonuses to his employees. Cayson dreams of a bigger office space for them all.

Somewhere between two dollars in his bank account and a two-million-dollar computer network contract, Cayson finds himself in the crosshair of the world's most notorious terrorist organization that is now coming after him, his business partners, his family, and even relatives he doesn't know exist.

Ignoring repeated warning lights might have been Cayson's downfall, but it's too late for him to backtrack...

The Crime...

Assigned to the National Cyber Investigative Joint Task Force, FBI Special Agent Stella Evans finishes assisting her colleagues from the Counterterrorism Division to apprehend a notorious terrorist.

On trial in Europe for war crimes too numerous to list, Molyneux refuses to help the authorities dismantle her sophisticated international computer network. The only alternative is to find the architects of this network and hope they will cooperate.

Shutting down Molyneux's underground computer network is the best way to destroy those mercenary terrorists for hire. However, the terrorist organization doesn't want to be outdone. A successor is named, and they begin to kill off anyone who has worked on the underground network in the past.

The Crisis...

By the time Stella reaches the Binary Systems global headquarters in Atlanta, Georgia, most of the original computer specialists who worked for Molyneux are either dead or have disappeared—except their fearful leader, Cayson Yang, the final link, kept alive for reasons unknown.

Stella finds herself at a crossroad between duty and following Cayson and the cybernetic implants in his head. She stands to lose not only her carefully cultivated career but, more dangerously, her closely guarded heart as she decides what to do with the Pandora's box she has opened.

Zero Sum (Binary Hackers Book 1)
JanThompson.com/zerosum

Binary Hackers
JanThompson.com/binary

To receive book news from Jan Thompson:
JanThompson.com/newsletter

ZERO SUM

PROLOGUE

"This better pay off, Kel," Cayson Yang said when his employee and friend came back to their booth at a corner of the noisy convention center. "We paid five thousand dollars for this spot, and nobody has stopped by all morning. Day two."

All around their tiny booth were gargantuan displays from mega technology firms that Cayson's small computer consulting company could never hope to compete with. They were big, loud, noisy, and they had food. Which Kelvin Gallagher had been munching on as he made the rounds, leaving Cayson to manage the Yottaflops Data Storage LLC booth on his own.

Kelvin had a mouthful of snacks. He muttered

something about missing breakfast. It came out sounding like he was missing *butter*.

Or *buffer*, depending on if you were at work or home.

"There must be hundreds of tech expos in the southeast, and we had to pick this one where we're invisible," Cayson continued.

"We? You picked it," Kelvin reminded him.

"Well, I'm scolding myself right now." Cayson pointed to one of the booths nearby. It had a big poster of a bobblehead advertising 3D printing, and a long wraparound line of people. "We're in the wrong business."

Kelvin pulled something from his pocket. It was a bobblehead doll of himself.

"Whoa. So that's what they're doing over there?" Cayson asked.

"Yeah. You can ask them to print anything for you. The kid in front of me skipped away with a nerf gun that actually shoots darts. I got this." He shook his bobblehead.

"You do have a big head. How much did it cost you?"

Kelvin winked. "If you have to ask, you can't afford it."

Across another aisle, speakers blared loud

Bollywood music as a huge crowd gathered around a demonstration of graphics design innovations.

Cayson felt the urge to get off his folding chair and join the decibels of success.

Instead, he found himself tidying his empty counter, stacking up business cards and a sorry brochure he had printed off their office printer—because someone had forgotten to order new brochures.

We're a digital company. We don't do paper. Save the trees!

The IKEA countertop was slightly chipped on a couple of sides from when he and Kelvin had tried to offload it from the top of his hybrid vehicle on Monday morning. That was after the Atlanta police had given him a citation for dangerous driving.

How was he supposed to know that bungee cords had a breaking point?

His D in college physics hadn't helped.

"Maybe we need a bowl of candy," Kelvin suggested. "Food draws people."

"Candy is not food."

"A technicality." Kelvin downed a whole bottle of soda and smacked his lips. "Maybe it's the name of the company."

"What's wrong with Yottaflops?" Cayson had picked the name of the company carefully.

At this moment in his life, yotta was the largest metric unit.

Hence, *yottaflops*.

A bazillion floating point operations per second.

Ten to the power of twenty-four.

That's some fast server.

"The dichotomy in meanings is too obvious," Kelvin explained, as if he thought that his employer had missed the point. "If we're not talking server speed, but data storage, it should be YottaBytes."

"But we're not only doing data storage," Cayson countered. "We do primarily systems. Systems mean servers, and servers means FLOPS."

Kelvin pointed to the logo on his bright-yellow T-shirt. "This says *Data Storage*."

"Whatever you do, don't talk to Leland about this. She's been wanting to fold Yottaflops into our parent company, Binary Systems."

"One name to rule them all..."

"She has fifty-one percent of the company shares. If she says it costs too much money to run two separate companies, then that's the way it is." Cayson looked around, wondering where all the customers were. "It has already cost too much money to change everything. Bank cards, logos, door signs, checkbooks—"

"Whoa. What? Did you say checkbooks? Who uses checkbooks these days?"

"I do. And I had them specially printed. A lot of money has gone into this business and we're still not breaking even."

Cayson had sold his house to start Binary Systems, Inc. Then he created a branch to give Kelvin a job. It hadn't seemed ridiculous at first because Cayson felt great saving Kelvin.

Thing was, Cayson was not Kelvin's savior.

But the deed had been done.

Binary Systems had spawned off Yottaflops, and now Cayson owed the IRS money.

The companies had to succeed.

Cayson couldn't live in Mom's basement much longer. Pretty soon she would ask him to do more than just take out the trash. At least she had not yet suggested that he volunteer in her law office in exchange for free meals.

Well, she had been taking care of his cats when he was at work all day and night long.

"Whatever," Kelvin said. "It's your company. Say, when is Leland coming? I have to get back to the machine room. Our Dubai client wants his data backed up somewhere safe and offshore."

"Hush."

"Like anyone can hear us—or even cares." Kelvin put up a palm. "Sorry. I didn't mean that in a bad way. Obscurity has its benefits, you know, especially in our line of work."

Cayson said nothing.

"I'll stay if you want me to." Kelvin wadded up another candy wrapper and tossed it into the trash can under the counter.

"I don't think we'll have a lot of foot traffic the rest of the day. Why don't you go?"

"See you at the meeting." Kelvin shook his head. "Who in the world calls for a meeting at three in the morning?"

Guilty as charged.

Well, when the customer was paying half their income, Cayson had no choice but to comply, even if they wanted to talk business at a time convenient to them. It would not always be during the day in Cayson's time zone.

The perks and perils of having global clients.

Cayson watched Kelvin go. He meandered in and out of the booths, picking up snacks, brochures, and such.

Kelvin was a hard worker. Not as brilliant a hacker as Cayson's cousin and business partner, Leland, but he was a great system administrator. And he didn't need any sleep. He could fill in all night long and still function in the daytime.

Boisterous cheering across the aisle from the Bollywood booth made Cayson look that way.

He flinched.

Blocking his view was a ghost from his past, gliding into his booth.

Startled, Cayson gripped the counter and felt the chipped edge cut into his palm.

He couldn't remember her username. He had only seen her online. Never in person.

Didn't she live in Asia somewhere? Macau someplace?

What was she doing in the United States?

Something must be terribly wrong for her to show up here. Why here? Why now?

"Are you Cayson Yang?" She sounded like she was in a hurry.

Her accent was pretty good. She had said online that she had learned English by watching American television shows.

But that was eighteen months ago.

No one was supposed to contact anyone else on the team.

They had all agreed.

What is she doing here?

Cayson decided he had to have a talk with Dmitri about this breach of security.

"Who's asking for him?" Cayson replied.

"Do you always speak in third person?"

"Huh?"

"Your name tag says *Cayson Yang*."

"Oh." Cayson winced. *Note to self: stop wearing name tags.*

"How may I help you?" He started over, continuing his charade. *Definitely need to talk with Dmitri about this.*

"I have a warning for Ulysses."

What warning? "You mean a message?"

"A warning."

Only a small handful of people knew who Ulysses was.

And even fewer people knew where he had gone.

In fact, Cayson himself had no idea where Ulysses was at the moment. Only Ulysses's best friend knew, and the latter was incommunicado.

Cayson prayed to God for mercy. He had thought that blighted time in his career was long gone. How could it resurface now, when he was trying to make a legitimate, aboveboard living?

"He no longer works for me," he said. "He's off the grid."

Bollywood music thumped in his ears. People cheered and made a lot of noise.

Cayson saw the woman's lips move, but he couldn't hear anything.

She came around the counter.

Cayson felt a sudden splash of spit or liquid or something on his face.

His eyes reflexively shut, and his shoulders pulled back. He lost his balance, and fell backward, going down on the carpeted floor.

As he rolled, he felt a sharp, quick stab just above his left ear.

The pain shot through his skull.

He screamed.

CHAPTER ONE

By the time FBI Special Agent Stella Evans arrived in Atlanta and drove to the VenomLabs office complex in Marietta, the third victim had been dead for almost a day.

Stella's flight from DC had been full, and she'd had to change planes in Charlottesville because of engine trouble. If anything could be worse, Atlanta traffic might rate up there.

From the Hartsfield-Jackson Atlanta International Airport to Marietta, the drive had been a crawl through rush hour in the metropolis, with the late-afternoon traffic going in the same direction she was, where Interstates 75 and 85 merged.

Her stomach rumbled for dinner that wouldn't

come for another couple of hours. But she couldn't worry about that now.

Three deaths in a week.

Today, it had been another network specialist of Binary Systems, Inc.

This time he had not died by his own hands. Jamal Cruze had been found in a roadside ditch in Woodstock, Georgia, some ten feet away from his Ducati.

His head had exploded under his helmet.

Officers from the Woodstock Police Department and the Georgia Bureau of Investigation had been all over the place. Their reports would be shared with her, she had been told.

Stella had no jurisdiction over the dead body itself.

But she had jurisdiction over the implants in the victim's head.

If her hunch was correct, the implants would be the same as those found on the other two dead employees, whom Binary Systems had contracted to the National Security Agency, two days before Cayson Yang had disappeared.

If she was correct, then she could safely say that they had all originated from the same implant prototypes stolen from VenomLabs two years ago.

New and improved and deadly.

Meant for the NSA, not global terrorists.

Grigori Norton had been the first victim, hit on the night of the data storage convention as he watched an evening cooking show at his rental apartment in Fort Meade. His housekeeper had called 911. Police had arrived to the gruesome sight of a headless body.

Six hours and a continent away, in the Binary Systems office in Prague, Audrey Lindberg had gone outside the building for a smoke. When she didn't return to the process her team had been in the middle of, they sent someone to find her. And find her, he did—her head splattered like a smashed watermelon on the old cobblestone sidewalk.

That had been the pattern of death: exploding heads.

So. Grigori Norton. Audrey Lindberg. And now Jamal Cruze.

As for another two hackers—Vivek Rao and Danika Svoboda—they were presumed dead, although their bodies had never been found.

Stella feared that the next person could be Cayson Yang.

Dispatched by the National Cyber Investigative Joint Task Force to Atlanta because her partner, Jake Kessler, had decided to stay behind in Fort Meade, Stella's job this week was to hang out with the cybernetics division at VenomLabs and make sure the FBI wasn't left out of the loop.

Of course, it had helped her cause that she had worked with Cayson Yang before in Project Pericarp, in which Binary Systems had been paid ten million dollars to set up an underground network for a supposedly British company so that the NCIJT could track the cashflow of terrorism.

Sometime this morning, the Cobb County Medical Examiner's Office had delivered the extracted implants from poor Jamal Cruze to VenomLabs. The implants had been badly damaged, but they were something to look at.

I suppose.

VenomLabs was the only contractor with the Defense Advanced Research Projects Agency. Whatever VenomLabs said, everyone believed.

Who watched VenomLabs, really?

VenomLabs owned a laboratory complex near the Dobbins Air Reserve Base in Marietta, just outside the Interstate 285 loop.

By the time Stella reached the front gate of the unmarked building, it was almost six o'clock. After this evening's meeting, she'd check into her hotel, get some sleep, and then drive to Chamblee the next morning, bright and early, for a NCIJTF meeting at the FBI field office.

For some reason, they didn't want to meet on-site at VenomLabs.

Something was off, but Stella couldn't put her finger on—

Her iPhone buzzed.

Jake Kessler.

The special agent in charge of her.

They had both been assigned to the NCIJTF, but Stella wouldn't do a thing unless Kessler gave her the all clear.

Stella sat in her parked car. She glanced around to make sure the windows had been rolled up. "Yes, sir?"

Excited about the NCIJTF collaboration with CIA field agents in Europe, Kessler was talking a mile a minute. All Stella could do was listen.

They had found Cayson Yang, and he was alive.

That was all Stella needed to know. "You want me to fly out to Istanbul?"

"Yeah. We have people keeping an eye on him, but they don't want to spook him," Kessler said. "A familiar face might help."

"What's he doing over there?"

"He seems to be checking items off his bucket list."

Yikes. "So that's why he's in Istanbul? Taking pictures?"

"He knows what we're up against. And we might be running out of time."

Stella had known Cayson for some years now. They had brushed shoulders again in recent months after the FBI had found out about the sale of MedusaNet to Molyneux's organization and had begun tracking their activities across the network.

Even with Molyneux on trial for international war crimes, there had not been any lull. Someone else had taken over the organization and was supposedly planning attacks on American soil.

Who is Molyneux's successor?

"If I fly out tonight, I'll be there tomorrow afternoon," Stella said. "Will I be too late?"

"Atlanta to Istanbul would take anywhere from twelve to sixteen hours or more, depending on how many stops you make."

Stella waited. She knew that Kessler would have a solution, or at least suggest options. He had been pretty determined to get Molyneux and had succeeded spectacularly—and in his own words, unexpectedly.

"I might have a faster way," Kessler said. "Pack your bags."

"My bags haven't been unpacked. I just arrived."

"Right. Wait for my text. I'll see if you can get a ride from Dobbins to Istanbul."

Dobbins Air Reserve Base was a couple of exits away from VenomLabs. Going against traffic, she could be there anytime Kessler wanted her to be.

"Who's going to babysit VenomLabs?"

"I'll take care of that. You and I will meet in Istanbul and go from there. And, Evans?"

"Yes, sir?"

"Trust no one. Not even me."

It was the strangest instruction Stella had ever heard.

CHAPTER TWO

When Cayson Yang stepped toward the tip of the rocky Trolltunga outcrop jutting out into the Norwegian atmosphere, the wind picked up, whistling a call for him to surrender to the depths below, a drop of some two thousand feet to the calming water of the lake Ringedalsvatnet.

How would it feel to be a part of the glacial lake of old?

Cayson inched forward on the flat granite top, his GoPro camera on a stick acting as a cover story for his venture into the dark abyss that had been crawling around in his head all week.

Like a thousand roaches, the throbbing darkness wove in and out of his brain, the implants giving no rest, no sleep, no peace, no future to speak of.

The last project had been his own doing and undoing—the payment of ten million dollars now a wasted bitterness on the tip of his own tongue.

He looked down at his grimy hiking boots, only inches away from the end of the world, beyond which was a vista worthy of award-winning photography.

Only he wouldn't live to see his future accolades.

Future?

There's none but more pain and sorrow, I tell you.

Cayson breathed in the crisp, clean mountain air sweeping through the most spectacular—and in his own estimation, the most picturesque—vista on God's green earth.

God.

Ah, forgive me, Lord Jesus, for my weakness.

I cannot take it any longer.

His cousin and business partner, Leland, might call him a coward.

I can't stand the roaches.

He had asked—pleaded, begged—for God to remove them, but the Almighty had not answered.

Why?

Who am I to order God around? To instruct Him?

Leland had often quoted Romans 8:28.

And we know that all things work together for good to those who love God, to those who are the called according to His purpose.

What purpose would it be to have inoperable implants in his head that could not be removed except by terminating his life?

And then what would Leland do?

Poor cousin Leland.

If I go, she'll be alone—

No.

She wouldn't be alone.

Leland was twenty-five years old. She could take care of herself. And Cayson's parents. And his cats.

Oy.

He had forgotten about his cats.

Well, Leland knew the routine. She'd make sure they'd be fed and happy.

Cayson had left instructions that his bots would deliver to Leland later regarding feeding his three cats—oh, and watering his greenhouse plants, especially the new *Nepenthes bicalcarata* carnivorous pitcher plants he had added to his collection.

All Leland had to do was make sure there was at least two inches of water in the immersion tray outside his flowerpots.

Oh boy.

Maybe he'd need to rethink this escapade. Somehow, he wasn't sure Leland would be in town enough to care for his parents, pets, and plants.

The more Cayson thought about depending on Leland, the more he remembered the nature of Leland's job. She often disappeared at a moment's notice, whenever the CIA called her to arms.

Intellectual arms, that was.

Flashes of light pulsed in his head again. He felt his brain rattle in his skull. The pain!

Aarrgghh...

The camera slipped out of his hand.

As he tried to pick it up from the granite, the pain in his head shot from one ear to the other, and he lost his balance, slipped on the rocky ledge, and fell...

Her screams lodged in her throat as Stella Evans sprinted toward the granite ledge and tossed the drone over the cliff as Cayson's shoes disappeared from her view.

Her heartbeat drummed in her ears, and she could barely think as she knelt down, her knuckles turning white against the remote control in her hands.

Please, God...

The wind was fierce, flapping her windbreaker against her back.

The small screen on her controller flickered to life, and she could see parts of the drone's extended claws.

In the speedy fuzz, Stella could make out the back of someone free-falling.

She held her breath as she watched the drone attempt contact, its claws reaching for Cayson's torso. The grip was clean and textbook.

The other camera on the back of the drone showed that the parachute deployed.

Stella's hands shook so hard that the screen on the remote control turned blurry.

"Let me," a male voice said.

Stella barely nodded as she handed the remote

to Jake Kessler, whom the military transport plane had picked up at Andrews Air Force Base on the way out.

En route to Istanbul, they had found out that Cayson Yang had bought a plane ticket for Oslo. From Oslo he had gone to Tyssedal.

Fortunately for Stella and Kessler, Cayson took over five or six hours to hike up to Trolltunga—a troll's tongue—thus giving the FBI special agents plenty of time to find a helicopter for hire.

Stella collapsed on the ground. Above her, the late-afternoon sky began to give up its light.

"He has landed." Kessler spoke into his wrist watch. "We're on our way."

He turned to Stella. "You okay? Deathly pale there."

"It's the sun."

"Right."

Stella closed her eyes and prayed that she'd stop shaking.

She had never been this nervous in her life. What was going on?

It couldn't just be Cayson, could it? Sure, they had known each other, but she had been careful not to get emotionally attached to a team member.

Besides, Project Pericarp had been over a while ago.

When she opened her eyes, there was one small, tiny speck of cloud in the distance. The rest of the stratosphere was denim blue.

It was such a pretty afternoon that it was hard to fathom that someone had just attempted suicide.

"We'd better get down there," Kessler said.

"Let him wait." And Stella meant it.

"He's by the lake."

"He won't drown himself. The drone will make sure he perpetually floats."

Still, there was Cayson Yang, somewhere on the grassy shore of a pretty lake directly below this ledge.

The somewhat suicidal Cayson was now America's only hope to shut down Molyneux's network used by her mercenary terrorists at large, now trading weapons with North Korea and Iran.

We are doomed.

CHAPTER THREE

"Inoperable! Do you hear me?" Cayson Yang yelled into the wind swirling around the vertical mountain walls around them.

A seaplane waited on the lake. He hadn't believed it when he had seen it land on Ringedalsvatnet only minutes ago, disgorging two ghosts—one from his near past and the other from his distant past.

Stella Evans nodded to him. "Calm down before you burst a blood vessel."

"Does that matter anymore?" Cayson tried to pry the six legs off his rib cage, but the drone held on. It gripped his torso pretty well.

And had saved his life when he had slipped off the rock.

He had almost changed his mind about jumping, but he had stepped too close to the edge, trying to retrieve his fallen GoPro.

Perhaps the wind had given him a push.

Stella was about six or seven feet away from him. She looked rather calm, having witnessed his ordeal.

Behind her, Jake Kessler stepped back, as if to give Stella space to talk a deranged man into going with them in that yellow seaplane.

"Cayson, remember me?" Stella asked.

"Why are you speaking so slowly?"

"Stella Evans."

"I know you who you are. You owe me coffee."

"I do?" Stella didn't seem to remember anything. "We can get coffee."

"Too late."

"No, not too late, Cayson." Stella took a step forward. Slowly.

"I'm not contagious," Cayson said.

Stella straightened her shoulders. "I didn't want you to do anything...uh..."

"Stupid?"

Stella spread her palms in front of herself. "Look, first we save the world. After that, what you do with your life is between you and God."

"I'm on death row, Stella. They're coming after

me—my head, specifically." He waited to see if the FBI special agent would correct him.

She did not.

He knew that she had remembered their friendship after the project had been over. She had insisted that he couldn't call her Agent Evans if they were going to talk about themselves.

She liked her coffee black with only a drop of whole milk.

"Arabica," Cayson said.

"You do remember."

"It doesn't mean my head's okay. They did this to us. In one week two of my employees have been killed."

"Three. They found Jamal Cruze yesterday."

"No..." Cayson's knees went weak, and he wobbled—

Whoosh!

The drone deployed an air cushion.

"Seriously?" Cayson began to laugh.

"That rescue drone is courtesy of DARPA." Stella pointed. "It's still experimental."

"Great." Cayson tried to get up. "I'll send them a thank-you note."

"The problem was finding you."

"Well, you did."

"We worked around the clock for a week," Stella said. "We couldn't find you for days."

"If you could hack into my implants, you would've found me."

Stella didn't respond.

"Oh. You did hack into my head."

"Technically, only your implants. VenomLabs has been testing ways to get them removed without killing you, but we need to get you to the lab."

"VenomLabs? The DOD contractor?" Why did a Department of Defense exoskeleton contractor have anything to do with...?

Oh. "Their cybernetics division. This belongs to them, doesn't it?"

Stella stepped closer. "They left their backdoor open and..."

"And Molyneux found the implants."

Stella nodded. "What they had installed in your team are not the prototypes anymore."

"I realized that."

"The implant from Jamal's head had Iranian codes inside."

"Iran?" *The plot thickeneth.*

"Who did you expect?"

"I don't care anymore. I have bigger problems." Cayson shrugged. "I tried to hack into my implants all week. It took out my vision one time, and then another time, I had such a bad headache I thought I was going to explode."

Kessler joined their conversation. "We will work on getting that implant out of your head if you help us shut down MedusaNet."

"You don't get it, Agent Kessler." Cayson moaned. "I've tried getting to MedusaNet all week. The closer I get to it, the worse my headache is."

Stella looked at her colleague. "So they're tied."

"What I need is a team of hackers to break down these implants," Cayson said. "But my teammates are all dead."

"Not all. We're your team," Stella said.

"We have hackers at the FBI Cyber Division," Kessler offered.

Cayson rolled his eyes. If they had been that good, the FBI wouldn't have had to hire out projects.

"We also have Raj Subramaniam's company, Rhinotec. They're on-site right now at VenomLabs."

Rhinotec was well known as one of the best computer security companies on this side of the world. Then again, the CEO himself had been the one saying that all the time, and Cayson knew he couldn't believe everything he heard.

"It's impossible," he concluded.

"Time to pray then," Stella said quietly. "You're a Christian. You know that nothing is impossible with God. If He wants you to live, you'll live."

"What if He wants me to die?" Cayson asked.

"Then you'll die. But it's not up to you, is it? Jesus is the One with the keys to life and death."

Cayson pointed a finger at her. "You're going to be fired for using religion on me."

"I'm on my way out, Cayson. This is my last project."

Before Cayson could speak, a flash of blinding light bolted through his eyes. It was so sudden, so violent, that he screamed and fell back.

"Now!"

Stella's voice came through the lightning in his mind.

Next thing Cayson knew, something pressed against his neck.

Whatever it was, it flipped off the bright light in his head. He was surrounded by complete darkness.

The world went still.

CHAPTER FOUR

Clayson woke up in a hospital bed in a room that smelled like toothpaste, for some reason. His senses were a bit messed up, to say the least, as he began to crave apples.

He blinked at the lights above.

This can't be heaven if it smells like toothpaste.

Or can it?

Somewhere, faintly, a familiar voice floated his way. It sounded almost like his mother's voice.

Mom. Dad. Are they safe?

He made a mental note to ask—

What is her name?

Inaudible voices—male and female—ebbed and

flowed in the room that began to look like a morgue. It still smelled like toothpaste.

He remembered his first computer repair job. Uncle Bobby down the street from his parents' home had owned a funeral parlor. He had an old 8088, and the floppy disk drive was jammed.

I kid you not!

Cayson tried to remember how long ago it was. He had been...how old? At this moment, he couldn't remember anything past yesterday. Even there, all he could recall was passing out by the lake from the pain.

Pain.

He felt no pain.

"Did someone give me a lot of painkillers?" Cayson muttered.

His headache was gone. For now? Forever?

He blinked.

Yep. No headache.

Quiet whispers reached his ears as he saw movement around him. They looked like ribbons of colors, kind of like when he looked at time-lapsed videos of city streets and highways.

"Try again." Another familiar voice. Male, this time.

"Checking the other nodes," the woman said.

Her reply seemed to come from above, like the

ceiling or somewhere high up there. Cayson wasn't
sure.

"Keep him awake," someone said.

"Is he going to be okay?" the female voice said
again.

Ah, Leland. Cousin Leland.

Why was she here? What did they want
from her?

*Leave her alone. She has nothing to do with
this!*

Leland would've been in Project Pericarp had
she not been called away, borrowed by the CIA to
solve some pressing issues in Rome, and then
borrowed again during her week off to help some
private investigator on an egg hunt.

Puzzle eggs.

Puzzle...

That's it—

A piercing pain behind his left earlobe short-
circuited his stream of thoughts. He couldn't hear
himself scream.

He tried to raise his arms.

They were restrained.

Before he could protest for his right to freedom
according to Uncle Bobby's interpretation of the
Constitution of the United States, the voices
stopped talking, his pain went away, and he faded

into a dream of stopping by the roadside to watch a funeral procession...

"There are so many layers around these nodes." Leland Yang-Joule pointed to the wall-mounted screen showing Cayson's brain in three dimensions.

Around her were VenomLabs cybernetics specialists, and Rhinotec hackers. The hands-on CEO of Rhinotec was also there. Raj Subramaniam had made it clear more than once that he wanted to buy Binary Systems and make the company a part of his growing company with "endless streams of work coming your way."

Sitting in the back, Stella listened to the flurry of discussions.

"He must've been out a long time for them to implant these things," Stella finally said as she stared at the image of Cayson Yang's brain. He was practically bionic.

Except all these cybernetic implants were probably killing him.

And the others before him.

"Kelvin is still missing," Leland said to Stella, as if the latter could do something about it.

You know, like save the world and all that.

I can do that. Piece of cake.

"If you're referring to Kelvin Gallagher, Agent Kessler is looking for him," Stella said.

"Technically, he works for a subsidiary of Binary Systems."

"I know. Yottaflops."

Leland nodded. "Cayson and Kelvin went to a data storage convention, but that was the last time Kelvin showed up for work."

Stella studied Leland. What was the hacker trying to say? She waited.

"I came on the scene when Binary Systems incorporated. Kelvin and Cayson went back a long way, way beyond Project Pericarp."

Stella figured Cayson must've told Leland a lot more than he should have. "What are you saying?"

"You know that Kelvin wasn't involved in Project Pericarp. Or do you know something we don't?"

"I don't know what I'm saying, to be honest, but if he has implants in his head—just like Cayson has —he might need help," Leland explained. "Just trying to be helpful."

"And we might have one more piece of the puzzle," Stella said, just before her phone buzzed.

She had to take the call.

The hackers started chatting again, and Stella excused herself to find a quiet place to answer the call from the special agent in charge, who had returned to DC for a special NCIJTF meeting at the Pentagon.

Her phone to one ear, Stella had barely reached the otherwise empty breakroom when she swayed. She leaned against the doorframe. "What? I thought he was recovering from the gunshot wounds."

"Me too," Jake Kessler said. "We're investigating."

"Of course." Stella's forehead rested on her palm. "Ben Quesnay. Wow. His wife has multiple sclerosis. Four little kids. I can't believe this is happening."

"We're setting up a fund for her and their children."

"That's the least we can do." Stella wondered how much she could contribute.

Single and unattached, she had very few expenses. Living on the road, chasing shadows, meant she had no mortgage payments to worry about. Once she arrived at the job site, all expenses were paid.

Her cryptology degree had helped in her job as a cyber special agent.

Somewhat.

She knew what the computer experts were talking about. Still, there were days when she didn't believe a word they said to her.

And she couldn't trust a thing the hackers did.

Unlike FBI Special Agent Ben Quesnay, who seemed to think that the entire Project Pericarp was connected to Russia's ФСБ—or FSB in its Romanized form.

Stella wasn't sure she shared his suspicion.

Project Pericarp had begun in the NSA, crossed over to the CIA, ricocheted through the FBI, and then returned to the NSA like a boomerang.

It had been over...

Or has it?

Clearly, elements of it had remained, like these various virtual networks that were spreading like cancer throughout the known Internet universe.

Well, the Federal Security Service of the Russian Federation were no doubt interested in Molyneux's underground network, but there had been no reason to think they were involved in helping maintain MedusaNet, which clearly had been owned by a British company before it had been sold to Molyneux.

And now we'll never know.

CHAPTER FIVE

"Icarus." VenomLabs chief scientist, Dr. Osman Reyes, walked around Cayson's bed, letting the other cybernetic researchers fill the room.

Cayson studied them, looking for familiar faces, but found none.

Where's Stella Evans? Leland?

Cayson assumed that either they knew what Reyes was about to tell him about Icarus, or they didn't need to know.

"Ah. So my implant has a name." Cayson drew a deep breath and crossed his legs. After sleeping here for several days, he had begun to like his bed and the nice one hundred percent cotton pajamas they'd been bribing him with.

"Implants. Plural," Reyes corrected him. "I didn't think anyone would survive with three, but you have five."

"Five implants?" Cayson tried not to move his head, in case doing so might dislodge something.

I don't know what it would dislodge—my brain?

"They form a helmet around your head and send you low-level electrical shocks now and then."

No wonder I keep getting headaches—I mean kept *getting headaches.*

"What did you do to make the headaches go away?" Cayson asked.

"They're not gone. We put some mini braces around your implants to lessen the stress on your brain."

"Oh, thank you, Doctor. I can always use less stress." Cayson looked at the others.

They said nothing to him. They stared at him, then jotted things on their tablets.

They might be doodling, for all he knew.

Reyes stopped at the foot of the bed. "We created Icarus for DARPA to test exoskeletons for supersoldiers."

The Defense Advanced Research Projects Agency had been researching strange and scary things since the late fifties. Cayson wasn't sure whether to feel honored to be in yet another

DARPA project or feel insulted that he had become a lab rat doomed to die.

"Two years ago, two soldiers were abducted in the middle of a live test," Reyes explained. "They were killed and dumped, but we never recovered our exoskeletons and their controller implants."

"And now they replicated those implants and put them in my team?" Cayson had always tried to be helpful. Maybe the good doctor could summarize all this and he could go home.

"Well, yes, but who knows how many of these next-generation implants they have mass-produced and implanted in people."

"Meaning?" Now Cayson felt uncomfortable, as though his bed was getting warmer.

"Meaning something is going on, and we'll get to the bottom of it."

I could have told you that, Doctor.

"My guess is it would have taken at least ten hours to implant them. But you said you don't remember any of it."

Cayson shook his head. "I remember falling asleep on the flight home from London. When I picked up my suitcases at baggage claim, I found that my entire team felt sick—headaches, nausea, aches and pains—like we were coming down with something."

Since they had gotten over all that a couple of weeks later, it had not dawned on Cayson that it had been anything other than a travel bug.

And then at the conference, Aspasia had shown up. What had she done to him?

Something was going to happen soon.

But what?

"As long as you stay here, they will not be able to access your brain," Reyes said. "This is your safe cube."

"Safe cage, you mean?" Cayson chuckled.

"Whatever you want to call it."

"Why can't you just surgically remove my implants?" Cayson asked.

"I guess you were asleep when we discussed this with your cousin." Reyes pointed to one of the cybernetics engineers.

The man cleared his throat. "Those third-generation implants have coiled around your blood vessels. If we try to remove even one, you could have a stroke or aneurism if we break a major vessel in your brain."

"And it's inoperable." Cayson hoped what he said wasn't true.

"If we can make them non-functional, they would be benign, just as they had been for months until someone showed up at the convention and activated them."

"So that's what that jab was for." Cayson remembered now. That day at the data storage convention, Aspasia had shown up, splashed his face with water, caused him to stumble and go down.

And then she had injected something into his head.

Something to activate his helmet?

"But they'll be in my head the rest of my life."

Everyone nodded at Cayson's realization.

"What happens when we've shut down their network? I can't stay in this cage forever," Cayson said.

They had no answer.

"Can I go home safely? Will they try to find me in five years?"

Reyes smiled. "You just focus on hacking into the MedusaNet. We will focus on hacking into your head. If we can destroy the implants without killing you, we'll try."

"I appreciate your honesty." Maybe. "When can I get to work?"

"One more day. Raj and your cousin can't wait for you to get to the machine room. Apparently, there are things that only you can do."

"Yeah. Like making a life-changing mistake."

"Technically, you created the MedusaNet for a British company. What they did after the completion of the work was entirely outside your control."

Reyes spread out his hands. "In the same way, we created Icarus for DARPA. When it was stolen, what the enemies did with it was beyond our control."

"But they sent it back to us, like a boomerang."

"That too." Reyes sighed. "Once they turned our state-of-the-art cyborg implants into kill switches, it became our problem again."

"Multiplied."

"Unfortunately."

Cayson knew that it would take tremendous resources to fix the problem of enhanced cybernetic implants now used on unsuspecting American citizens—implants capable of turning heads into fireballs.

And he would be the first in a long string of experiments to find out how much it would cost the taxpayers.

"So many laws have been broken," Cayson said. "I didn't ask for these implants. It was against my consent. I would never have voluntarily subjected myself—or my team—to this."

Reyes nodded.

Something he isn't saying.

"I don't envy you, Dr. Reyes." Cayson stretched his legs. "I don't envy you at all."

CHAPTER SIX

"How are you doing?" Stella stood by Cayson's hospital bed, her arms folded.

"Feeling more like my old self again," Cayson said.

Leland walked in. She must have heard his remark. "Lazy and doing nothing, as per usual?"

"Wish I could do that," Stella said.

Cayson moaned. "Feel free to take my implants."

His cousin waved her hand in an arc in front of his face. "When you blink, are you taking our photos?"

"Like this?" Cayson blinked furiously.

Leland and Stella both covered their faces.

Cayson laughed.

Someone called Leland's name. Raj peeked in through the door. "Machine room. Pronto."

"On my way in a sec." To Cayson, Leland said, "Be ready, cuz. We're going to hack into your head tonight."

Cayson groaned. His cousin was a better hacker than he could ever be, but even the best could fail. If they failed, his life was on the line.

No wonder Stella had made him sign those stacks of forms from the government.

If you help us, you will die.

If you don't help us, we will all die.

Either way, Cayson felt that he was the only person who was doomed.

In the end, Molyneux's successor won.

"Have you found out who this understudy is? The one taking over MedusaNet?" Cayson gently tapped the edge of his bed.

Stella responded by sitting down in the recliner on the other side of the bedside table. She leaned back and closed her eyes.

"Tired?" Cayson asked.

"Yeah. But I'll get up in a minute." Stella stretched her arms over her head. "I came to tell you that your parents are safe. The GBI has a few safe houses all over the state."

Cayson had not had any encounters with the Georgia Bureau of Investigations, but he was glad that both the federal and local authorities were helping his family.

My tax dollars at work. "How about my cats?"

"All accounted for."

"Thank you."

"And your neighbor says he'll check on your carnivorous plants, in case they need more water. He says he'll send you the bill later."

"And he will." Cayson interlocked his fingers over his chest. "I wish... I wish we had gone for our annual physicals more regularly so that these implants could've been discovered sooner before we're all killed."

"You're not dead yet."

"My colleagues, friends, employees are."

Grigori Norton.

Audrey Lindberg.

Vivek Rao.

Danika Svoboda.

Jamal Cruze.

There had been nine of them in the Project Pericarp operation. Those five, plus Dmitri, Ulysses, and Cayson.

Kelvin hadn't been invited.

But Kelvin was currently missing.

Is everything connected?

Cayson prayed that God would protect Kelvin, wherever he was.

"Maybe it's time to start over," Stella suggested.

Cayson nodded. "Lotsa flops the last several years for Yottaflops. Wish I never chose that name. Binary Systems, Inc., sounds more benign."

Benign.

The same word that Dr. Reyes had used this morning when he had come to see his only patient in the entire VenomLabs complex.

Well, to be sure, Reyes was a cybernetics scientist and not a medical doctor per se.

And Cayson felt safe here for now because Reyes had told him he was.

"Can they read your thoughts?" Stella pointed to her own head.

"Not through my implants."

"Why not?"

"The implants are kill switches."

Kill switches.

The same phrase that Reyes had used in their last conversation.

"We don't know that yet," Stella countered. "Raj tells me it will be weeks before they figure it all out."

Then why had Reyes made it sound like he had been certain?

Are these implants really kill switches?

Stella kicked down the footrest and stood up. "When you feel better, let Raj know. He has two teams in place—one to hack into your head and the other to hack into MedusaNet."

"I'm not sure if we should do it at the same time."

"We don't have time to do anything. Kessler informed me that we now believe the possible attacks on cities are going to be homegrown. Travel restrictions basically prevent any importation of outsourced evil," Stella said. "Which city? When? Those are real problems."

"I guess they're bigger than my headache," Cayson offered.

"I'm sorry. I didn't mean that."

"Seriously, I hope we make it through." Cayson coughed. "I want you to know I'm not usually suicidal."

"It only takes one time," Stella said.

"I'm sorry."

"It's not your fault that those implants are in your head. Frankly, I'm surprised VenomLabs couldn't extract them already, considering they invented the prototypes. I think a surgical robot could cut the coils around those blood vessels."

"Not easily," Cayson said. "It would've been easier for me to..."

"Don't go there, Cayson."

"I couldn't even kill myself."

"Matthew 10:30 says, 'But the very hairs of your head are all numbered.' God gives and takes lives, not us." Stella bristled. "You're still alive because you have a job to do."

"Molyneux's successor."

"We still don't know her name. We're thinking it could be her other daughter."

Cayson nodded. "I'll be curious to know who this understudy is."

"We're still shutting down the network, regardless of who's in charge. MedusaNet had caused troubles on both sides of the Atlantic with its liberal use of private VPNs. Organizing terrorist attacks or mass protests had never been easier."

"Easy for you to say, Stella. I'm stuck, you know. To shut down MedusaNet, we have to get close to it. If we go near it, I die. If we don't, I also die."

"I'm sorry."

"Nonetheless, I don't want to be stuck with Icarus the rest of my life. It would be like that movie, *Groundhog Day*. Imagine an Icarus replay every day."

"You meant redux? Icarus redux?" Stella asked.

"No. Replay." Faintly, Cayson heard audio. "Did you say something?"

Stella shook her head. "I do need to get back to work."

"Babysitting a bunch of hackers?" As Cayson said it, he was listening to Icarus whispering in his ear.

Replay ready. Listen?

Cayson waved to Stella as she left him alone in the room.

Following the same pattern, Cayson replied to his implants. "Icarus, yes."

Dr. Osman Reyes's voice and his own filled his ears.

When the replay reached the two words again, Cayson froze.

Kill switches.

Reyes had mentioned kill switches while VenomLabs and Rhinotec were still investigating what those enhanced and heavily modified implants were supposed to do.

To call them kill switches would be premature and inconclusive.

Does Reyes know something no one else knows?

CHAPTER SEVEN

"Wow. You've been through a lot." Byron Moss, the counseling pastor from Cayson's church, sat back in the chair he had pulled up against the hospital bed.

"That's just the gist of it." Cayson looked across the railing of his bed, toward his friend and confidant. "It's money, isn't it? Makes me do things."

"Money is amoral and apolitical. The Bible says that it's the *love* of money that traps people." Byron opened his Bible, as he often did.

Cayson waited.

"1 Timothy 6:10 says, 'For the love of money is a root of all kinds of evil, for which some have strayed from the faith in their greediness, and pierced themselves through with many sorrows.' Don't confuse loving, wanting, pursuing money with the object of money itself."

Cayson nodded.

Five million dollars said it was his love of money that had indirectly caused the death of three people in a week.

Byron should know of what he spoke. While he might be a humble Bible teacher and a patient counselor at Midtown Chapel, his family history in the Bahamas was not born in humble circumstances.

They were well-to-do, and yet Byron and his wife lived in a modest house while giving away a lot of money to church ministries and charities, such as scholarships for Bible college students.

Cayson wondered how much money it would take to sway Byron.

As for Cayson, he could say that it took very little to push him this way or that.

Five million dollars had done it. It hadn't been much if he added up the payroll taxes, annual taxes, overhead, capital, employee salaries. Why, there'd be a pittance left.

Then again, if he had known that the Virtual Private Network, and in fact, the entire company, would then be sold to a terrorist organization, Cayson wouldn't have taken the money.

Too late now.

Three people were dead.

"It took us three months to construct the network because the British company wanted the VPN to be strong enough to withstand FSB hackers," Cayson said. "That should've been a flag, but I didn't see it at that time."

"I'm not sure if you should drop entity names or tell me that much detail," Byron said.

"A dead man's confessions, padre. Give me that."

"All right. Go ahead."

When Cayson finished with all the lurid repercussions of having a past project come back to haunt him, Byron suggested they pray. It was a short prayer because they were running out of time.

Cayson wished he hadn't been that talkative, but Byron was the only one he could confide in—other than God Himself.

When Stella had suggested that Cayson talk to a counselor about his pilgrimage to Trolltunga the week before, the first person who had come to his mind was Byron. He had moved to Atlanta after his marriage, and finished his master's in counseling from Midtown Chapel Bible College, a ministry of their own church.

"Sometimes we make decisions in a fog," Byron said. "Pray that God will clear the fog and show you the path to walk on."

"I see now that decisions really do affect the rest of my life."

"Having said that, we also know that God has much mercy for our mega messes."

Cayson nodded. "In other words, God's mercy cleans up our messes."

"Speaking for myself, I am a person in need of constant forgiveness," Byron said. "May I never be arrogant about my own deficits."

"Me neither."

"You know, recovery is as important—if not more important—than discovery."

Cayson chuckled. "You going to write a devotional?"

"I could."

"Put all these nuggets in. I'll buy a copy."

"Whew. For a moment there, I thought you might want a free book."

"I could, but then nothing is free. Either I pay for the book or you do," Cayson said. "Even my salvation in Christ is not free. Jesus paid it all."

"Amen."

CHAPTER EIGHT

*'m so dependent on technology that I forget I
am but dust.*

Monitoring the activity log for the
hackers was not something Stella had expected to
do. All around her, people were chattering away
and hammering on those poor old keyboards.

Stella stayed in the machine room all day long
with the dozen hackers whom Raj Subramaniam
had brought from Rhinotec, several hackers from
DARPA, and still more from VenomLabs. Thanks
to some sort of agreement that had been made prior
to Stella's arrival at the VenomLabs complex, Raj
was in charge of the lot.

It turned out that Raj's company was a

contractor at VenomLabs, though they had arrived after those supersoldier implants had been stolen from a US Army laboratory in Maryland.

Remembering what Kessler had told her made Stella pay more attention at VenomLabs.

Trust no one. Not even me.

In the last two days, she had submitted multiple requests for background checks on everyone at VenomLabs, from Osman Reyes down to the night-shift janitors, from front-desk receptionists to back-room hackers.

No one had been spared.

Hailing from Madrid, Osman Reyes had a Canadian mother who still lived in Toronto. His graduate and postgraduate work had been dubious, but he had won enough awards to cover up any glitches in his curriculum vitae.

Still...

At four o'clock in the afternoon, Stella looked up from her scrolling screen to find Cayson Yang staring down at her. He looked a bit pale, but there were bright lights in his eyes.

"How was the meeting with your pastor?" Stella asked.

"One of the pastors from church. We had a good discussion."

"Glad to hear that you're on the mend. Any headaches lately?"

"No. But I'm still not sure if I'm ready to be hacked." Cayson sat down on a nearby chair.

"You're afraid these hackers could kill you."

"Not intentionally, but by accident. And being dead isn't as much a worry as being alive with a stroke or a preventable ailment."

"You would trust God for that, right? Our lives are in God's hands."

"Indeed. He's the only safe place," Cayson said.

T he pulses in his head made Cayson cover his ears, as if that would help. It did not.

The pulses increased until he heard a voice in his ear.

Stop!

Cayson couldn't believe it.

Icarus, is that you?

No response.

Well, I suppose we're not there yet. No wordless human-machine interface at this time.

"Icarus, report." Cayson kept his voice down to almost a whisper.

Surprised that he had eased this quickly into managing his implant, and suddenly protective of the app inside his head, Cayson wondered if there was a way to protect Icarus from external interference.

He spun around in his chair and faced Leland on the other side of her workstation. "Was that you?"

Leland looked up. "Me what?"

"Did you try to hack into my implants while I wasn't aware?"

"If you weren't aware, why are you talking about it?" his cousin asked.

"Someone just tried to hack into—wait. I'm not sure anymore." Cayson turned toward Raj. "Is everything secure? Any third-party hacking going on?"

Raj checked. "Not that we know of. Besides, we tried accessing your implants this morning. It failed, remember?"

"Yeah."

"So until we have new algorithms, we probably won't try again. Besides, you're in a safe place here, so we're not worried about your head exploding like a pumpkin all over the place."

"Yikes, Raj. Remind me not to go to work for a man with a morbid sense of humor."

"How did you know something was happening in your head?" Raj sipped his coffee.

"I heard a voice say *stop*." Now that he mentioned it, it sounded foolish.

"That gives new meaning to a voice in your head," Leland said. "Are you sure someone was trying to access Icarus? What if it's just you getting too close to MedusaNet, thereby triggering something in your implants?"

Raj came over to stare at Cayson's workstation. "How far did you go?"

Cayson had nothing to hide. He pointed to a window. "I'm almost at the DMZ."

"And you only worked on this for a few hours?"

"He's fast like that," Leland said.

Cayson didn't respond. He'd had a bit of help.

Still, he wondered if they were really safe.

"Someone outside could have been trying to access my implants," Cayson suggested.

"You keep thinking there's a third party," Leland said.

"I don't know—"

Boom!

The building shook.

Boom! Boom! Boom!

The walls cracked, and pieces of them fell off.

As if by instinct, Cayson crawled under his steel workstation.

Above him, the ceiling caved in on top of the hackers.

In the chaos of painful screams, all the lights went out.

CHAPTER NINE

"Leland!" In the pitch-black darkness, Cayson tried to get oriented.

Leland is that way, isn't she?

Cayson started walking. The ground was uneven. He stubbed a toe on something that felt heavy and concrete. "Leland!"

"I wish I had a flashlight." On a whim he said, "Icarus, flashlight."

And there was light.

Stunned, Cayson froze in his steps.

The faint glow from his head grew brighter, casting a pale-green light on the rubble on the floor.

Cayson told himself he'd look in the mirror later. For now, he had to make sure Leland was alive.

Being five years older, Cayson felt responsible for her well-being.

"Leland!" Cayson called out again. "Lord Jesus, where is my cousin?"

"H-here!" Leland raised a hand out from under her table. She was wincing. "My foot is under the rubble."

They had both thought of the same thing: take cover.

Only problem was that Leland had not been fast enough.

Cayson prayed that she had not crushed her foot. He carried concrete rubble away from the table and the bent ergonomic chair.

"Can you move your foot?" he asked.

"I don't know. I shouldn't have worn sandals."

It was too dark to see if Leland's foot was bleeding. It all looked green to Cayson.

Icarus was a night light.

"Eeeek! Cayson, you're glowing green!" Leland's voice was shrill.

"Technically, he's only glowing in five spots," Raj said.

"Cayson! Leland! Raj!" Stella's voice came through a hole in the wall where the door once had been. A bright flashlight beam penetrated the dusty clouds floating in the room.

Moans and groans were heard all around. Raj's hackers scattered all over the room needed help. But first, Cayson had to get Leland to safety. Then he'd come back to assist the others.

Raj yelled back to Stella. They both made their way to Cayson and Leland.

Leland was wincing and limping out of the rubble.

"Get Cayson out of here," Leland said through gritted teeth.

Cayson reached for her arm. "We're all going."

"No. I think my foot is broken—or sprained badly." Leland held her breath, but tears began to flow. "Agent Evans, please get my cousin out of here. It's him they want."

"This could be an earthquake," Stella said.

"Metro Atlanta is on a bedrock. Earthquakes are very rare," Raj said. "I'm thinking we got bombed or something crashed on our building."

Stella shrugged. "I've called 911. The firefighters and paramedics should be here soon."

"Leave now, Cayson," Leland said as Cayson and Stella escorted her out of the destroyed machine room. "If they're after you, you're not safe in this chaos."

"I can't leave you, cuz."

"I can't go with you. My foot is hurting something fierce. I need to wait for the paramedics."

"I'll stay with her," Raj said.

"I don't know..." Cayson looked at Raj and then back at his cousin.

"I'll be fine. We'll sort this out and we'll regroup."

Cayson wanted to ask her how she thought they were going to get back together. But Leland answered before he could pop the question.

"Old MacDonald," she said.

Cayson let go of his cousin.

Old MacDonald.

He hadn't expected that they would need his help so soon. To find him, Cayson would have to go to a certain place in the woods of North Georgia and wait.

He wasn't sure if he wanted to do it. "I don't know where he is."

"Where the deer roam."

No way.

I can't believe Old MacDonald hasn't left Georgia.

"Go." Leland made eye contact with her cousin. "Now."

Cayson nodded, but his legs didn't go.

"We'll get your mom to safety."

"My cats?"

"Yes, your cats too."

"And my plants?"

"I'll water them." Leland cringed and reached for her foot. "Go before we all die."

Cayson nodded again. More often than not, he trusted Leland's judgment. If she said they needed Old MacDonald, then she knew something Cayson didn't.

"Since there's no electricity, the safe cage is gone," Leland continued. "Molyneux can find you now."

"Molyneux's successor," Cayson corrected her.

"Which could be anybody, really."

"How are we going to defeat an unseen enemy?" Even before Cayson thought about his own question, a name came to him in a quiet whisper in his head.

Mole Rat.

Midnight without electricity in the VenomLabs compound was as dark as pitch tonight. With Cayson's implants turned off so as to not attract too much attention, they had to rely fully on Stella's flashlight to find her vehicle in the parking lot.

When they reached the car, Stella found herself staring at a jam-packed parking lot filled with vehicles trying to get out of there. In the distance, car headlights showed her that the gate was locked.

Without any electronics, there was no way the gate was going to open, unless someone rammed it.

No one wanted to sacrifice their vehicle—or airbags—for it.

There was no way to get the car out of the VenomLabs parking lot. Even if they drove to the back gate, Stella could see a swarm of vehicles already moving that way.

Two gates and hundreds of cars.

VenomLabs was open around the clock, and researchers often stayed for long hours.

This was the price to pay.

Car horns of all decibels mixed in with shouts asking the night guard to manually open the gate so people could leave.

There had to be a manual override somewhere, but Stella wasn't sure she wanted to wait around.

"Let's walk," Cayson suggested.

Stella swiped her iPhone. It was still working. "I'll call the field office to send us a vehicle."

After hanging up, Stella told Cayson that they'd get their new vehicle at a gas station down the road.

They scaled the fence, rolled down a landscaped slope, and started walking.

The entire area was dark. No traffic lights. No street lights. No moonlight.

That told Stella that their enemies didn't only bomb the building they were in, but also did something to the surrounding area to prevent anyone from escaping. Would they return to finish them off?

"They didn't use EMP," Cayson said. "Icarus is still in my head."

"I agree. If they did, you'd probably be dead now." Stella said it first before she believed what she said. After the Trolltunga rescue, the last thing she wanted was to lose Cayson to an electromagnetic pulse bomb.

"More than likely, they took out the electric grid." Cayson pointed to a wreck at an intersection where the traffic lights were out.

Distant police and ambulance sirens drew nearer.

"Why use such a primitive method?" Stella asked.

"Icarus, explain." Cayson's voice was a whisper.

Stella waited.

Cayson shook his head. "Icarus says human psychology is not his department."

Stella laughed. "I don't think you should tell him to deduce and guess. That might scramble its circuits."

"You don't sound worried."

"Because humans are the resilient ones. If I were to guess, Cayson, I think they took out the electric grid because they want a functional Icarus when they find you."

Cayson flinched. He hastened his steps.

"This way." Stella stopped at an intersection.

They weren't wearing reflector vests. By the grace of God, they were not run over as they jaywalked across the street toward the gas station. Stella's flashlight helped.

When they reached it, the gas station was dark and silent. There was movement inside the convenience store, but the door was locked.

"Bad news," Stella whispered. "I don't see any vehicle anywhere."

"Maybe they're out back."

Stella shook her head. "Maybe we don't want to use a company-issued vehicle, you know?"

"I agree. I think God is protecting us from being tracked."

Stella knocked on the glass pane on the door.

The man inside, standing at the counter in the dark, didn't move.

Stella lifted her FBI badge and shone her flashlight on it.

Still, the man didn't move.

"Help us!" Stella mouthed.

The man ambled around the counter, something long and large in his hand.

It looked like a double-barreled hunting rifle.

"What do you want?" he said from behind the locked door, weapon pointed at Stella.

"Water and a Georgia map," she said as clearly as she could through the intercom.

"Money?"

Stella pulled out some twenties and tens. She had about a hundred dollars of spending money she could flash. She pressed the bills against the glass.

He seemed satisfied.

Just as he unlocked the door, bright and high headlights swept across the entire front of the gas station as someone opened fire.

CHAPTER TEN

"**G**et inside! Get in!" Mr. Shotgun shouted at them as he unlocked the door.

Stella got off the floor, and covered Cayson's head with one hand, pushing him inside. When Cayson looked at her again, her other hand was holding a Glock pointing away from him.

Mr. Shotgun locked the door and ushered them to the back of the convenience store. Down a long hallway they went, with Mr. Shotgun locking what looked like a series of fireproof doors. Perhaps they were thicker than that. As they went further behind the store, the noise from the front entrance subsided.

"This is a long hallway," Cayson said.

Nobody replied.

Cayson wondered what that man was going to do to them.

Enemies came in two sizes: the bad, badder, baddest.

Okay, three sizes.

Cayson was sure that his tenth-grade English teacher would have failed him two times out of three for not using the comparative worse and superlative worst.

But when life and death were at stake, who had time to speak properly?

"We better get out of here before they come around the back," Mr. Shotgun explained. "I don't have ballistic windows in the back, and that's where I parked my truck."

"You're not going with us," Stella said.

"All we want is a Georgia map," Cayson said. Paper maps didn't require a battery. He knew where they needed to go, even though he hadn't told Stella. She'd just have to trust him on this.

"Map?" Mr. Shotgun scratched his few-days-old beard.

"Yeah, a paper map. Do they still print those?"

Mr. Shotgun went to a desk, pulled out drawers until he found a crumpled old map of Georgia, folded incorrectly, torn in a couple of places. "Fifty dollars."

"Say what?" Stella's jaw dropped.

"Supply and demand."

Cayson took the map from him. "This is not even a new map."

"It's Georgia. Landscape hasn't changed since 1732, young man." Mr. Shotgun stretched out his palm. "Cash, please."

"Unmarked bills?" Cayson asked.

"If you have any."

"I don't carry cash."

"No cash, no map." Mr. Shotgun dropped the worn-out map into the drawer it had come from.

"Wait," Stella said. "I showed you a stack of twenties earlier."

"Sixty dollars then."

Without arguing, Stella gave him three twenties.

Cayson grabbed the map before Mr. Shotgun changed his mind.

"We'll also need food, a tote bag, some batteries, two ponchos," Stella said.

Mr. Shotgun didn't move. "Why you running if you're the law, ma'am?"

"Why you carrying a shotgun, sir?"

"Protecting my store." He flexed his arm.

Cayson saw a tattoo just above his wrist. He recognized the pattern. He pointed to Stella. "She's also a Marine."

"Yeah?" The man's eyebrows rose. His eyes fixed on Stella.

"Semper Fi," she said.

"Well, then." Mr. Shotgun dug into his pockets. Dangled the keys in the air.

Truck keys.

"You're going to let us drive your truck?" Stella asked.

"You need a vehicle. I'm serving my country."

"And if anything happens to the truck, you claim insurance."

"That too."

Stella drove the rusty old truck that smelled like leaking oil because she was afraid that the Icarus implants in Cayson's head might have other ideas for their trip.

She reached for the air conditioner, and realized it didn't work. There was duct tape over the glove compartment because the latch was broken.

No wonder Mr. Shotgun gave them the truck

key. He wanted to collect insurance. Maybe he'd get himself a new truck.

Then again, who was Mr. Shotgun? When they were climbing in the truck back at the gas station, Mr. Shotgun kept watch until they left his parking lot through a back road. Was it possible for a Good Samaritan to appear out of nowhere to help them escape their active shooter?

Stella stopped herself. There would be time for forensics and analysis later. Right now she needed to thank God for delivering them from the lion's mouth.

Lord Jesus, I don't thank You enough.

"Me too," Cayson said. He began to pray, and Stella waited until he finished.

"Amen. Now tell me where to go," Stella said.

"Dahlonega."

"Where?"

"I forget you're not from around here. Take Interstate 75 and keep going until we get to 575."

"What's in Dah..."

"Old MacDonald."

"I heard Leland mention that back at Venom-Labs. What did she mean?"

Silence.

"Cayson?" Stella knew he wanted to trust her.

Cayson started shutting down his iPhone.

"Shut down your phone. Better yet, we should throw them all out."

"Wouldn't it be enough to shut them down?" One hand on the wheel, Stella's other hand reached for her phone. She tossed it to Cayson.

"Not to Mole Rat…"

"That's some name."

"Or Molyneux or whatever. Creatures of the grand sewer."

Stella reached Interstate 575. "Take that road?"

Cayson nodded. "We'll go through Holly Springs, Canton, Ball Ground, Dawsonville, then Dahlonega."

"How long?"

"An hour and a half."

"Then what?"

Silence.

"You know you can trust me."

"I don't trust myself," Cayson confessed.

Stella had heard that before. It had been a warning from Jake Kessler.

Trust no one. Not even me.

Stella had half-expected to be shot at the gas station. How did their attacker—intimidator—know where to find them?

Stella had only called the FBI field office in

Chamblee. No one else knew where they were heading.

"Something is out of place," she said.

"Because we survived?"

"Because they let us live." She almost shrieked when she saw Cayson toss their phones out the window.

"If we survive this, we both get new phones," Cayson said casually. "I could use more memory in mine."

"That's my work phone."

"Ah, even better. If there's a mole in the FBI, they can't follow us now."

Makes sense.

"And one nice thing about old trucks... No one can hack into it."

"No Wi-Fi." Stella smiled. "But oh, the irony."

"What?"

"Icarus."

That was all she had to say.

Cayson groaned. "They'll find us sooner or later. We need to get to Old MacDonald fast."

"There you go again. Care to explain?"

"Old MacDonald is Leland's mentor."

"Never heard of him before."

"After this is over, you won't hear from him again."

Why not? Stella decided not to push. The truth would come out later.

"Do you know how to use a gun?" She asked instead.

"Sure. I was a paintball champion back in college."

"Did you say *paintball?*" Stella pressed the gas pedal, and noticed that there was only a quarter tank of gas in this old Toyota pickup truck.

"Those were the days." Cayson nodded, some distant, undecipherable happy memory etched on his face.

"I bet." *We're dead.*

CHAPTER ELEVEN

Outside Dahlonega, Stella stopped at the first gas station that came into view. It was almost two in the morning, and Cayson was asleep in the passenger seat.

She filled the tank quickly, paid for it in cash, drove off to a more secluded, less well-lit parking lot, and woke Cayson up.

"Where to next?" She handed him a bottled water.

"We'll have to hike. I'm not sure if we have enough water and food."

"Hike? We're unprepared. Why can't we drive?" Stella asked.

"Because I don't know where Old MacDonald's farm is. We'll need to get directions from someone."

"Who?"

"I don't know his name."

Normally, Stella considered herself to be a patient person. Tonight, all that went out the window with Cayson and his head—potentially waiting to explode.

"I'm wearing flip-flops," Cayson said.

"Brilliant."

"We'll have to stop somewhere to buy me some closed-toe shoes."

Stella sighed. "Wonderful. We're going shoe shopping right in the middle of an assassination attempt."

"You're referring to the vehicle that showed up at the Marietta gas station, so quickly after the VenomLabs machine room was bombed into ruins and the city electrical grid taken out."

"I'm sure they weren't shooting the breeze."

"I wonder who Mr. Shotgun is," Cayson added.

"Never look a gift horse in the mouth."

"Unless the gift horse is a Trojan house."

Stella stifled a smile. "Very clever, Cayson, or is it Icarus being witty tonight?"

"It's me, Stella." Cayson's voice sounded

pained. "It's still the same me you knew from three years ago."

The one whose dinner invitation I turned down several times.

Stella had nothing more to say to Cayson.

He could talk to Icarus.

She just wanted some peace and quiet.

The last day of her job couldn't come fast enough.

I don't need this.

"You want me to drive?" Cayson asked. "Get some sleep. I'll wake you up when we get to the trailhead."

"Should I?" Stella asked, blinking.

"Your eyes are about to close. I know the general location of where we need to go. You don't."

"You said Dahlonega." Stella yawned.

"Even though it's a small town, it still has many roads. Besides, we're not going through town. I'm going to circle around to the other side of town, where there is a rural road leading to Old MacDonald's farm."

"I wonder if you're making all this up." She swerved. "Sorry. Rabbit on the road."

"There was no rabbit on the road." Cayson's voice was alarmed. "Pull over, Stella, because you get us all killed."

All? Funny how he should include Icarus.

"Icarus is not a person," Stella said as she put on the blinker and eased onto the emergency lane.

At the edge of the forest north of Dahlonega, Cayson parked the truck on the gravel between the road and a kudzu-covered ditch.

Stella stirred. "We're there?"

"No. We're here. *There* will take us maybe a whole day of hiking."

She unbuckled her seat belt. "We start now?"

Cayson nodded. He stepped outside the truck and lifted one foot in the air. "New hiking boots. I checked your boots and they're nice combat boots—where did you buy them, anyway?—so I figured you can hike in those. So I only bought myself a pair."

"When did that happen?"

"While you were sleeping. I also bought us two backpacks, sleeping bags, snacks for our journey, and bunch of camping gear."

"Sleeping bags? Camping gear? We're just going to hike one way."

"Better safe than sorry, my mother always

reminds me. By the way, I kept everything under two hundred dollars."

"How did you get all these under two hundred?"

"A twenty-four-hour Walmart around the corner, at the edge of Dahnolega. Discounts galore."

"But you told Mr. Shotgun back at the gas station that you didn't have any cash."

"I used your money."

"You took it out of my pocket?" Stella's eyes widened.

"You still have several hundred-dollar bills left," Cayson said. "Besides, you said to go ahead."

"When?"

"An hour ago."

"Wait—you had a conversation with me while I was asleep?"

"At that time, I thought you were awake— maybe barely, but you conversed with me."

"I don't remember anything."

"You need a memory upgrade." And Cayson laughed all the way to the back of the truck.

Stella followed him. "I can't believe I talked to you in my sleep."

"I can ask Icarus to—"

Oh. Cayson really didn't want to tell her that

Icarus could replay their entire conversation. He'd do that only if Stella insisted.

Stella.

She had been Stella since the end of Project Pericarp, when she had arrived to replace the agents fired for dereliction of babysitting duty, though that very term had insulted Cayson.

We hackers don't need babysitters.

"You owe me a cup of coffee, Stella," Cayson said.

"Did you buy a cup just now? With my money?" Stella asked.

"I should've, but that's not what I meant. You do know what I meant."

Stella glanced at her watch. "What kind of food did you get?"

"We'll have doughnuts. Good day or night."

"Seriously? You should've woken me up. We'll need protein though."

"You looked exhausted. Plus, we'll be hiking all day, and I didn't want you to pass out from the heat."

"What?" Stella stepped toward Cayson. Her eyes came up to his cheeks. She jabbed his chest with a finger. "You stop insulting me. I might be a city girl, but I know what a hike looks like. I've been a Girl Scout. And I saved your life on Trolltunga."

Jab. Jab.

Cayson was suddenly speechless.

He placed his hand over hers.

And she pulled away.

The moment was lost.

Without a word, they unloaded the two back-packs off the truck. Cayson tied their sleeping bags to their respective backpacks.

Cayson told her to step back. He climbed into the truck, and eased it slowly down the ditch. The incline was steeper than he had expected, and he had his boot on the brake the whole time. The truck rolled to a stop between the road and grove of kudzu-covered trees and bushes.

Putting it in neutral, Cayson gave the truck a little nudge, and it rolled farther into the forest and disappeared into the trees, completely covered by the ivy-like kudzu and the dark shroud of the night.

He stood next to Stella, who was checking her watch. "Four o'clock in the morning, and we're going to hike in the dark. How are we going to find the truck later?"

"If we succeed, we won't need it later. We'll be home free."

"Then we're littering."

"It'll surface in the winter when the kudzus die out."

Ping!

Startled, Cayson froze.

Attempted access on Icarus detected.

"Icarus, who?" Cayson asked.

Point of origin unknown.

Before Cayson could say a word, Stella was already hoisting her backpack over her own shoulders. She helped Cayson with his.

He tried to speak.

"Shhh. Talk later. Let's go." She stepped forward. "Which way?"

CHAPTER TWELVE

Three hours after they had begun hiking, the sun rose above the trees, revealing that they were all alone in the forest. No road signs. No directions.

It surprised Stella that Cayson knew where to go at all, but she wasn't one to question Cayson's judgment when she had no options to offer. Besides, she suspected that Icarus was his GPS.

She prayed that they hadn't been going around in a circle, because geometrically and geographically, they could very well return to where they started. Then what?

Cayson led Stella further into the dense forest, and then north toward who knew where. "We'll stop for breakfast soon."

"I never pegged you as a hiker," Stella said.

"Desperate times."

"Truth, though?"

"I was a Boy Scout. We hiked and camped a lot. You?"

"Yes, I told you, didn't I? However, truth be told, I'd rather spend time in the chess club."

"Never pegged you as a chess player." Cayson looked around. "How about here?"

"How long are we stopping?" Stella took off her backpack, and massaged her shoulders.

Then she looked for her phone. When she couldn't find it, she remembered that Cayson had gotten rid of it.

"Ten minutes if we can eat fast."

"What do we have for breakfast?"

"Granola bars." Cayson handed her two.

"Thank you. All I need. I'm on a diet."

When they sat down to catch their breath, the echoes of broken twigs in the distance seemed to freak out Cayson. He wanted to leave.

Then Stella saw a deer. She pointed.

"For real?" Cayson bit into his granola bar.

Stella said nothing.

She listened for unusual sounds, knowing that she was outside her element. She had not chased criminals through such forests and over uneven clearings where there could be black bears and copperhead snakes and suchlike. Stella's environment was the city. City streets, backroads, alleys. Those were her jungle, her forest.

Not this.

She half expected to hear gunshots in the air, but she knew their pursuers would not make that much—

Noise.

And then she heard it.

It was the sound of a drone coming closer, weaving in and out of trees.

Cayson's eyes widened, and Stella could see the white of his eyes in the morning light.

They grabbed their backpacks and ran.

"Molyneux sent a drone to Santorini to chase after some people Leland worked with last year." Cayson spoke as calmly as any running man could.

"Anyone hurt?"

"I'm not privileged to see the full report, and I don't know the PI who witnessed the event, but Leland said the drone was armed."

"If they send a drone, it'll whizz through the forest faster than we can run, with all this undergrowth."

Cayson nodded. "And my hiking boots are brand new."

"You bought thick socks?"

"Yep. Should help, but normally, we would be hiking, not running through the forest with loaded backpacks on our backs."

"Normally? Has anything been normal the last several years for you?" Stella asked.

They continued to run due north until Stella could not hear the drone—or drones—anymore.

Insect sounds rose like choruses as the sun grew brighter in the sky. The trees around them provided canopy and shade for them as they trekked through the forest, heading north.

A trail appeared with wooden signs saying that somehow if they hiked that way and over there, they could magically end up on the Appalachian Trail that stretched all the way from Georgia to Maine.

Stella didn't feel adventurous today.

She felt hungry, like she hadn't had enough breakfast. "If we lose them, let's stop for—"

The engines were loud, but the rapid gunfire was louder still—and fast approaching them.

"Hide!" Stella pulled Cayson along. They leapt over a fallen and decaying tree trunk, and tumbled down a slope that ended at a tiny stream.

The leaves and branches stirred above them,

sunlight peeked in, and Stella could see sparkles in the water. Specks of gold?

They crawled to an overhang where tree roots jutted into the air and downward, looking for soil.

Stella threw off her backpack, and Cayson followed her.

They packed themselves into the crevices among the roots of an overturned tree and the other trees perching precariously at the edge of the river.

Stella glanced back to see a flash of metal heading their way, coming through the trees.

How many drones are there?

"I see only one," Cayson said.

"How about you run one way, and I'll go around it and shoot it down?" Stella asked under her breath.

"You mean I'm bait?"

"It won't be easy." Stella pulled her Glock out of her waist holster. "Have you ever done skeet shooting?"

"All you have is a Glock. You don't have a hunting rifle."

"All I have to shoot is the CPU."

Cayson kept his voice down. "All we have to do is survive."

"And I'd rather survive with you." Stella froze. *Did I say that?*

"We're quite a pair, Stella. We didn't die three years ago, but we just might this time."

The thought of it saddened Stella.

"Stella?"

She looked up.

Cayson had that look of intensity that Stella had seen when he was deep at work on solving a problem.

"If anything happens to me, I want you to know that I wanted to have coffee with you but didn't have the guts to ask."

Stella opened her mouth, but before she could say a word, Cayson suddenly fell over and wailed as his hands clutched his head.

Above them, Stella saw the drone coming.

It had found Cayson.

It looked unarmed, but that wasn't its purpose, was it?

Stella left Cayson on the ground by the river-bank. She dashed behind another tree and checked her Glock. She figured she could take out the drone if it came closer.

Fifteen feet.

Cayson was writhing in pain, rolling on the muddy bank.

Stella could not bear it.

Please, Lord, help him!

She held her Glock in her two hands, like any normal day at the practice range. She hadn't missed in the last five years, and she wasn't about to now.

The drone swooped down.

Stella aimed and fired.

CHAPTER THIRTEEN

"We have a long way to go before nightfall," Cayson said. He still felt a numbing headache from Icarus screaming in his head earlier. Nonetheless, they had to press on while it was still daylight.

"We got attacked two hours ago. Let's rest a bit."

Stella seemed to be able to keep up with him even though she carried a backpack weighed down with the remains of the destroyed drone sans GPS, which Cayson had removed.

"On the contrary, because we've been attacked, we need to keep moving." Cayson tried to ignore his headache. "They know we're here now, and they will send another drone. This time we may not be able to shoot it down just like that."

Icarus had probably gone to sleep, as Cayson hadn't heard from it in the hours that they had been on this hiking trail. They ate lunch on the trail, sitting on rocks along the way, and kept hiking. By late afternoon, Stella seemed a bit antsy.

"Where are we going?" Stella asked. "You still haven't told me."

She was right. Cayson hadn't said anything. Should he now?

"There's a hunting cabin up ahead on this trail. That's the beginning of several parcels of private land," he said. "We can take a lunch break there."

"A cabin. Good idea."

"There's no furniture in the cabin," Cayson warned her. "It's just pine flooring."

"I don't care. It's not like we're going to spend the night there."

"If we are, we have sleeping bags."

Ping!

This time, Icarus was speaking gibberish. There was no language in there, only jumbled noises and an occasional snort.

"Icarus, reboot." Cayson didn't know what else to say, really.

In under a minute, Cayson heard from Icarus again.

Icarus system rebooted.

"Good." Cayson chuckled. "Icarus, my personal butler."

I am not butter.

"Poor thing. I think Icarus is broken."

I am not bokeh.

They reached the top of a small clearing, where a bench told them that this was not an isolated hiking trail. However, the path was getting narrower and less visible. In some places, the trail disappeared altogether.

Up ahead, Cayson saw more signs.

Private Land.

Keep out.

The temperature was cooler under the tree canopies. It was still September. The leaves had not changed colors. Yet.

The rustlings of leaves made Cayson turn. "Look, Stella, a squirrel."

On ordinary days, this would have been a common sighting. But Cayson had gone through a lot.

His free will had been violated by cybernetic implants.

His company had lost so many employees that

he had no idea if they could ever be a company again.

And Stella.

When he had first met her the year before, they had talked some. That had been all.

Now he found her fascinating.

He checked to see what she was doing.

She looked a bit tired.

"Want to swap backpacks?" Cayson asked.

"No need. We don't want your headache to return."

"It won't."

"No guarantees."

"There are no guarantees in life."

Stella nodded. "No. Did you know that we lost another agent last week? He was following an FSB lead. Left behind a wife with MS and four kids. How sad is that?"

"I'm sorry. Was it something I did?"

"Was it?" Stella shrugged. "At this time, I think it's unrelated, but he was outed by an agency mole. I don't know if the mole is aware of Project Pericarp."

"Speaking of 'wife and kids,' have you ever thought of...maybe someday settling down?" Cayson measured his words carefully.

"When I was studying cryptology in the Naval

Academy, I had no idea I'd be an FBI agent. So I suppose anything can happen." Stella stopped to catch her breath. "I suppose the best thing to pray about is for God's perfect will to be done."

"When I did computer science in college, I didn't know I'd turn into a cyborg."

A cyborg.

A cybernetic organism.

"Maybe when this episode is over, DARPA can figure out how to remove Icarus from your head."

"More experiments. I'm afraid I'm damaged goods."

"Only your brain." Stella laughed so hard it echoed all around. She cupped her mouth with her hands to stifle her laughter.

"I see it's an inside joke." Cayson put on a frown. "You're the only one laughing."

"Be serious." Stella cleared her throat. "Don't forget that once we shut down MedusaNet, to which Icarus is tied, then you'll be free."

"You think?"

They came across a cliff with trees and a small view of the distant mountains.

"Nothing like Trolltunga." Cayson pointed to the sun, dipping in the sky.

"Is the cabin far from here? The sun will set soon. We need to conserve our flashlight batteries."

"Stella?"

"Yes?" Stella was standing on the trail, watching Cayson inch toward the edge. "Maybe you shouldn't stand that close to the…"

Cayson smiled. "You're worried about me."

"No. Just concerned."

"Come here."

"What for?"

"Come see the sunset with me."

"When will that be? Maybe we shouldn't stay put in one place for long."

"It'll be all right."

Stella didn't move. "I'm sweaty, sticky, and I don't want to stand next to you right now."

"Come here anyway."

Stella ignored him and started walking.

Cayson had no choice but to follow her. "Cabin's maybe fifty feet away. There's a well behind it, and we might be able to get some water to boil."

"Boil with what?" Stella asked.

"I bought a single-burner camp stove, a cooking pot, and a frying pan." He patted his backpack.

"What's in mine?"

"Shower kit, water purifier, and some other stuff."

"Well prepared, are we?"

"I just went to the camping aisle at Walmart and packed up."

"With my money." Stella chuckled.

"Technically, we're at work. Operating expenses."

Cayson saw a part of the cabin roof. "There it is. When we get there, we wait for someone named Tyrone to show up."

"Who told you that?"

"Leland. That's what she had to do the last time she came to see Old MacDonald."

He doubled his pacing and Stella followed, but before they reached it, Cayson stopped and put his arm in front of her.

The windows reflected flickers of candlelight inside the log cabin.

There was laughter. There was conversation.

The cabin was occupied.

CHAPTER FOURTEEN

To Stella, Cayson looked distressed. He had brought her here to this secluded cabin so they could take a break before continuing their hike at sunset and dusk through the forest toward a specific GPS coordinate where they would receive directions to Old MacDonald's farm.

And someone else was in it.

"I'm blanking out," Cayson said. "I only remember that several of us were allowed to use it any time. Ninety-nine percent of the time it's unoccupied."

Stella prayed about her next move. If they had wandered to the wrong cabin, then where on earth were they?

"So we knock on the door and get some info," Cayson asked. "Is that what you think we should do?"

"No. I don't think we should talk to strangers right now."

"Give me a minute to think." Cayson retreated to the base of a tulip tree. He sat on a protruding root.

The front door swung open.

The business end of what looked like a Weatherby Vanguard Series 2 pointed in Stella's direction.

"Looking for someone?" the bearded man holding the rifle asked.

Stella put her palms up, one hand holding her weapon. "I'm Stella, and this is Cayson. We were told we could use the cabin anytime."

"I don't know anything about that. We live here." Mr. Weatherby pointed his nose at Stella. "Lower your weapon to the ground."

Stella complied.

"Now kick it toward me," he said.

Stella complied again.

"How long have you been here?" Still sitting under the tree with his arms in the air, Cayson didn't sound panicky.

Mr. Weatherby laughed. "I do the

questioning."

"I was told the cabin is rarely occupied," Cayson pressed.

"We've been here for six or seven years."

"That long." Cayson's voice deflated.

Stella turned to Cayson. "Maybe we found the wrong cabin."

"Could be. They build them all alike," Mr. Weatherby said.

"May I stand up?" Cayson asked. "I'm not armed."

Mr. Weatherby nodded slightly.

Cayson inched forward. "I'm looking for Old MacDonald."

"We don't know anyone by that name." Mr. Weatherby still had not lowered his Weatherby. That wasn't very friendly of him.

"Is there a campsite around here where we can stay the night?" Stella prayed for the right words to say. "We're on a hiking vacation, and we might have wandered off the beaten path."

"A vacation with a Glock. Interesting."

"Self-protection."

"There's a stream two miles from here. A picnic area with some clearings you can pitch your tent."

He had assumed tent, and Stella, too, had assumed Cayson had a tent. She glanced at

Cayson's backpack. Would he have been able to fit a tent in that space? Maybe. Probably, if the tent was small.

A two-people tent. Stella wasn't sure what to think of that.

But first...

"May I have your name?" Stella asked.

"No."

"Then I'll keep calling you Mr. Weatherby."

A twinkle appeared in the man's eye. "You have a Weatherby?"

"No, but my dad does. He hunts for elk sometimes."

"Elk. Someday. You go with him?"

"No. I don't hunt for animals." Stella smiled.

"She hunts for people," Cayson said. "Oops."

Mr. Weatherby's eyes steeled. "What kind of people do you hunt?"

Stella glanced at Cayson. *You put your foot in your mouth. You deal with this.*

Cayson cleared his throat. "The same people Old MacDonald does. We need his help to stop some terrorists."

"Ah, terrorists. To some, they might be freedom fighters."

"Well, it does depend on whom they terrorize, but if you must know, at this time they're terrorizing the United States. Since you live here, you're going to be affected."

He didn't move. "It still doesn't explain why you're here, ten miles into the forest."

"Wow. We're ten miles in?" Cayson seemed genuinely surprised. "I thought we'd hike more than ten miles."

"Ten mikes from the nearest town."

"Oh. Then again, since we had to run, we probably covered a lot of ground—probably not in a straight line."

"Run?" Mr. Weatherby asked. "Why are you running if you're the hunters?"

"Did we ever say we're hunters?" Stella asked. "We'd better go if we want to find that picnic area in the daylight so we can pitch our tent."

"Oh... About that..." Cayson looked at Stella sheepishly.

"What?"

"I only bought what I thought we needed. I was sure we'd be in a cabin, so I did not buy a tent."

"And here I'm thinking you bought a tent that folded up so small it fit into your backpack."

"No."

"What if it rains?" Stella asked.

"It's not going to rain," Mr. Weatherby, said. "The forecast said it'll be muggy all afternoon and then cool tonight. Start yourself a campfire at sunset, and you'll be fine."

"I'd like to have my Glock back," Stella said.

"No." Mr. Weatherby continued to point his weapon at them.

"It's mine, though."

"I confiscated it."

Stella decided it was probably foolish to argue with the business end of a rifle.

"Now leave before I give you bullets for souvenir." Mr. Weatherby waited until the duo walked away.

Stella made a mental note of the cabin and the man. The FBI could go after him to get it back. It was as simple as that.

"I don't think we should go to the river he told us about," Stella said.

"I'm sorry I suggested knocking on the cabin door." Cayson's shoulders slouched.

"We didn't. He saw us coming."

Cayson nodded.

"Now where is the real cabin we need to go to?"

"I don't know anymore. I'm not even sure where we are."

"Didn't you ask Icarus?"

Cayson flinched. "I think he's sending a homing

beacon."

Stella should have expected that. If Old MacDonald were to help them at all, they shouldn't lead their enemies to their only hope, right?

"I'm not sure what to do," Cayson said.

"We press on. We find Old MacDonald and hope he disables your homing beacon before our enemies show up."

Enemies? Actually, there was probably only one: the next Molyneux.

And of course, as they walked, it rained. The rain soaked through their clothes and shoes, weighed down their backpacks, stirred up mud on the trail, and ruined their evening.

In the heavy downpour, they trudged on until they reached another cabin.

"That looks like the last one we just visited," Stella said. "Mr. Weatherby's cabin."

"Didn't he say they're all the same?"

"Yeah."

"Should we check?"

Stella was thinking when she noticed something from their vantage point among the trees.

There was a small wall lantern sconce to one side of the door, illuminating the porch.

The cabin door was ajar.

"Stay here and wait for me," Stella ordered

Cayson.

He nodded.

Weapon out, Stella walked slowly to the cabin.

At the door, she saw Mr. Weatherby on the floor, a bullet hole in his forehead. Nearby, a woman and three kids were sprawled out on the single-room cabin, laying in pools of blood.

All looked dead.

S tumbling on the uneven forest floor, Stella and Cayson ran for their lives away from the log cabin house of horrors, their screams still lodged in their throats. Above them twilight turned into dusk and then night.

Under dark clouds and forest canopy, rainwater ran down the forest floor in torrents. Stella kept losing her footing, as her boots wanted to go with the flow of the runoffs.

Cayson gripped her hand as they continued running to who knew where.

Approaching an incline, they both slid down the muddy trail, never letting go of each other's hand, lest they lost the other in the night, too dark to be seen without a flashlight.

When Stella had seen the butchery, she had

never screamed louder. She knew the rain would mask her voice, but the picture in her mind could not be erased.

Stella had not wanted to disturb the crime scene. But she had seen her confiscated Glock on a wooden table in front of the fireplace. So she had tiptoed in, past the bodies, to retrieve it.

As she scrambled back to where Cayson was hiding, she thought she dropped something, but it wasn't her Glock. She saw something fly away from her into the bushes, but she could not tell what was there since it was dark.

There was no way she was going to dive into the bushes now to search and recover what she had dropped. She had to get Cayson to safety.

Whatever she had dropped, they'd have to do without it.

No loss compared to what had happened to Mr. Weatherby's family.

Slaughtered like livestock, he, his wife, and their three children hadn't stood a chance.

The killing was too brutal, too precise, too planned.

Planned.

Programmed?

Who—or what—could have done such an inhumane thing?

CHAPTER FIFTEEN

"**D**o you think they'll come back for us?" Cayson asked as they slowed down to catch their breath.

Nobody seemed to be following them. They needn't have run amuck.

Could they go back to their picnic site? Should they?

Flashes of lightning gave them light and showed them how far they could go. To be sure, they had stayed on the hiking trail so that even if they couldn't find their way, they wouldn't be completely lost in the woods.

A series of thunder and lightning later, Cayson could hear sizzling crackles of nearby trees getting hit by lightning.

The thunderstorm had morphed into an electrical storm, which continued as Stella and Cayson went along the hiking trail that meandered through the forest.

The noisy rain, peppered by occasional thunder and lightning—

What's that buzzing noise?

Cayson glanced back, but it was impossible to see into the rain that had drenched their faces.

He felt a strong tug as Stella tripped, pulling his arm with her. They tumbled down the winding trail. Unable to get up due to the muddy water, they slipped and fell again.

A bright flash of lightning covered the area, showing tall trees on both sides of them, and ahead, a V formation of drones hovering in the air, with little turrets pointing in their direction.

"Uh-oh. Stella?"

"Run!"

Cayson's heart rapped against his chest wall as he tried to remain calm for both of them. He and Stella had held on to each other for support to prevent themselves from falling badly on the muddy hiking trail and breaking bones.

He ran forward in his rain-soaked brand-new hiking boots, keeping pace with Stella. They found themselves by a mountainside, where cliffs were everywhere. There was no telling how far the muddy water beneath their shoes could take then down slippery slopes.

Whenever lightning flashed, they glanced back to find the drones still chasing them down.

Suddenly, a barrage of gunfire surrounded them.

Stella pulled Cayson to the ground.

Lord Jesus, we're going to die!

~

Well, they didn't die.

Thank You, Jesus!

While Cayson and Stella crouched behind either a sweet gum or tulip tree—Cayson couldn't tell which one it had been—their rescuers showed up.

They found themselves surrounded and delivered from the kill zone by none other than Robin Hood and his merry men—and women—who had appeared out of nowhere and had gone skeet shooting on those killer drones.

It turned out the stranger's name wasn't Robin Hood. It was Tyrone.

Cayson remembered something about him.

Leland had mentioned that the way to Old MacDonald was via Tyrone and his prepper group.

Tyrone had arrived in the nick of time, but how? In any case, Cayson and Stella had no choice but to follow them through the forest to an enclave.

If he had to backtrack, Cayson couldn't begin to tell how they had left the forest and somewhat arrived at this community of cabins surrounding a common area.

The rain subsided enough for Cayson to see that Stella was in a mess. She had cuts and bruises all over and particularly nasty gashes on her forehead and arms from when she had slipped and fallen in the forest after they'd left Bob's house.

Bob. That had turned out to be Mr. Weatherby's real name.

Tyrone knew who that man was.

That meant Cayson had probably arrived at the right cabin after all, but could not convince Bob to help them. He had sent them away.

"Stay away from the whole area until we've assessed the situation," Tyrone said. "We have many unanswered questions. But for now, take a shower, eat some food, and get some rest. You'll be in my cabin. My son is about your height. His clothes should fit you."

"Stella?" Cayson watched an elderly woman escorted a limping Stella away from him.

"She's going to stay with Alicia, just a few cabins down. Alicia is our nurse practitioner, so she's in good hands."

"I don't want us to be apart." There, he'd said it.

"Are you two married?"

"No."

"Then you'll see her tomorrow morning, bright and early. Soon enough for you?"

What could he do? These people were armed.

Cayson nodded.

Stella could take care of herself.

"What about our backpacks?" Cayson asked.

"When we have inspected them, we will return them to you."

"Fine."

As Cayson followed Tyrone to his log cabin, he wondered how the drones had found them.

Icarus.

It was obvious.

"The drones could come back," Cayson said. "They now know where to find Stella and me. Your entire village is at risk."

"We're not a village. Only a community." Tyrone unlocked his front door. "We'll deal with the drones in the morning."

"What if they come back tonight? Before dawn or something?"

"Obviously, night comes before dawn." Tyrone almost laughed at Cayson.

"I wanted to get my point across. It's life or death." *Either way, death for me.*

"We'll talk in the morning." Tyrone invited Cayson into his cabin.

His wife wasn't around, but she had left some clothes and blankets on the living room futon.

"Not to worry," Tyrone said. "We have twenty-four-hour security here. We'll shoot down any drones that come to this private property."

That makes me feel better.

"The question some of us have started to ask is, why are the drones after you?"

Cayson drew a deep breath. "I'm not sure they want us dead just yet. Maybe not until after they get what they want."

"Hmm... The fact that they were shooting to kill negates your statement that their operators wanted you alive."

"Wait. What?"

"They weren't trying to capture you. They left the same marks inside Bob's cabin as they did on the trees when they missed you."

"There you go. They missed us."

"On purpose, you think?"

"If that's the case, they did not try to kill us," Cayson reasoned. "Perhaps they tried to scare us."

It made no sense, but Cayson was fresh out of ideas. He dared not think that the drones could get whatever they wanted out of him even if he were dead—

Icarus.

Do they want Icarus?

If that were the case, the drone operators could not be working for VenomLabs. VenomLabs had a chance to extract Icarus out of his head but they hadn't done it.

"My entire community is now at risk," Tyrone said. "Should we trade you for provisions for the families living here?"

Cayson's jaw dropped. "I'm sorry."

Tyrone held up a hand. "I made the decision to go in and extract you two when the security cameras showed the squadron of drones."

Who owns those drones?

Could a third party have injected themselves into the project?

CHAPTER SIXTEEN

J ust after dawn, Stella woke up to find her eighty-nine-year-old host, Alicia, reading her Bible, and then starting to sew clothes using an antique Singer pedal sewing machine.

During off hours, she was also the community nurse, as she had demonstrated with the stitches on Stella's forehead and arms the afternoon before.

Sitting in a small armchair, Stella leaned toward the old handheld mirror that she had borrowed from Alicia. The gash on her forehead would eventually turn into a scar, but at least the wound hadn't been worse.

She glanced at her left arm. Six stitches. Earned on the slopes of mud and madness.

The evening storm was still fresh in her mind, even though it had been at least nine hours ago.

Alicia covered up her sewing machine. "Ready for breakfast?"

Stella nodded. She followed the elderly woman out of the cabin.

"I'm going to the kitchen." Alicia pointed to a building. "We cook breakfast for everyone."

"May I help?"

"No. I don't want you busting those stitches on your arm."

"Thank you for taking good care of me."

"Don't mention it. I'll see you in the pavilion." Alicia disappeared into the community kitchen.

Stella stood in the open field and breathed.

The mountain air was clean and refreshing this morning. All was quiet and tranquil. Stella shouldn't have a single care in the world, save for all the death and destruction that waited for her once they left this Still Waters Community.

In the meantime, this was their retreat. Their time-out.

"Hey."

Cayson's voice carried in the wind toward her.

When she turned around, his jaw dropped. "That looks painful."

His gentle fingers touched her forehead just below the stitches.

"I'll heal," Stella said.

"It'll leave a scar." He thumbed her lips.

"A war trophy."

"A memory." He lowered his lips toward hers.

She didn't protest.

In fact, she wanted more. She wanted him to kiss her this way the rest of her life—

What am I thinking?

When they came up for air, Cayson asked, "And your arm?"

Stella lifted it slightly and winced. It felt stretched. She dropped her arm down again.

Cayson looked down. "Wow, Stella. You look like a pioneer woman with that long, *flowy* skirt."

"I don't think *flowy* is a word."

"Flowing. Whatever. The calico flowers look pretty on you."

"Thank you." Stella had worn skirts sometimes, but Cayson had probably never seen her in one. On the job, slacks with holsters worked better for moving in and out of elevators and small spaces.

"How much sleep did you get?" Cayson asked.

"At least ten hours. I slept well on a cot. You?"

"I could have had that much if Tyrone's dog

hadn't licked my face and woken me up." Cayson laughed. "I was on the couch."

"Somehow I feel tired, like I need to sleep for two days or something."

"We've been through a lot."

Stella started walking. "You ready to have breakfast with a bunch of strangers?"

"I feel bad that we're bringing danger into this place. They didn't ask for it."

Stella nodded.

"Leland told me that Tyrone can take us to Old MacDonald," Cayson whispered. "Good thing Tyrone found us. I had no idea where we were going."

"You confessed all that yesterday."

"I did?"

"Don't tell me that Icarus is making you lose your memory."

"Tiredness and exhaustion can make me forgetful too." He held her hand. "But I won't forget our time together."

"Neither will I."

After breakfast, no one left the covered pavilion with its long tables and benches. It could have easily seated a hundred people, so Stella figured they probably had room for expansion.

Most of the people here were at least in their forties and older. There were a few people who looked like they could be in their thirties. Perhaps the kids had finished eating and left the pavilion.

Table talk included how to preserve and store food for nuclear winters.

Nuclear winters?

"Tell us your story," Tyrone said to Cayson.

Oh boy.

Stella waited to see how Cayson would respond. Here they were, in the midst of fifty strangers.

Cayson stood up. "How much should I tell? You're all strangers to me."

"We're not strangers anymore," Tyrone said. "We saved your life—and hers—yesterday."

Cayson nodded.

"Besides, you're trespassing on private property. A thousand acres of these mountains are ours free and clear. You brought death to Bob's family by passing through."

"I am so very sorry." Cayson's voice cracked. "However, you saw the footages. The drones killed them. The question is why."

"Let's start with this." Tyrone seemed to be genuinely trying. And to be enormously patient with them. "How in the world did you end up here? We bother no one. We just want to live in peace."

"What have we ever done to you?" someone said, dabbing her eyes. "We don't even know you. Now Bob, Maya, and the kids are dead."

Cayson's shoulders drooped. "We came to find Old MacDonald."

"Old Mac?" someone answered.

Tyrone lifted his hand. It must have been a signal for them not to disclose any more information than needed.

So they do know who Old MacDonald is. Perhaps also where he lives.

That confirmed what they knew about Tyrone.

Stella waited.

"Until we see him, there's not much we can tell you about who we are," Cayson said. "I can tell you that our presence here truly endangers your lives. If you can just point us north, we'll be going on our way."

"Oh, a quest."

Then the barrage of comments exploded.

"He doesn't need any help. Arrogant millennials!"

"What sort of kids are they raising these days?"

"He probably doesn't have any useful skill!"

"Annoying brat!"

Cayson cleared his throat. "I'm right here. Sort of..."

"Can you shoot? Hunt? Fish?" a booming voice asked him.

"Uh... We have grocery stores for that," Cayson said.

They all laughed.

"Poor kid. He'll never survive out in the wild."

They laughed again.

"Out here, God's nature is our grocery store," Tyrone said quietly.

"You don't seem to raise a lot of chickens, yet you cooked at least sixty eggs this morning," Cayson said. "Where did you get those eggs?"

"Oh, he's thinking. Questioning." Tyrone smiled. "I like that."

Some wheel noises made Stella turn to see two teenagers with one wheelbarrow each, filled with parts from last night's drones.

"No!" Cayson visibly freaked out five ways to

Christmas. "You do not want to bring those in here. They have GPS. All of you are in danger."

"We already were," Tyrone said. "Our societies are in ruins. Shambles. Freedom is at stake. We are already in danger. The end is near."

"Did I mention those things have GPS?" Cayson tried again.

"We killed them," one of the teenagers said.

"Sure. You smashed up everything?"

"We could use parts for our radio projects," the other teenager said.

"Ah..." Cayson looked at Stella.

"You could reconfigure them," Stella said.

"I'm not a drone expert." Cayson scratched his head.

"But Old Mac is," Tyrone said.

CHAPTER SEVENTEEN

Cayson and Stella rode their borrowed bicycles behind Tyrone for about five miles across hiking trails further into the forested private property. Then they had to walk their bikes along a stream, being careful not to lose their packs of damaged drones strapped to their bikes and in their backpacks—which Tyrone had inspected and returned to them after breakfast.

Minus Stella's FBI badge.

Cayson remembered Stella talking to Tyrone about their backpack inspection. It might have been her head injury, but Stella couldn't remember if she put her badge into her backpack, or whether she had dropped it in the forest.

To Tyrone's credit, he offered to search the

bushes around Bob's cabin, hoping to find her badge.

The trio came to a stream. It was clear and cool and looked perfectly fine to drink from, but Tyrone had advised both of them not to. They were down-stream, he said. And there were many deer upstream from here. They got the picture.

Cayson drank filtered and boiled water from his water bottle. And so did Stella.

Her arm muscles were in pain and giving her fits, and the most powerful painkiller they had at the community was Tylenol. Halfway through this forest, Cayson had offered to carry her backpack on top of his own.

Cayson had not dared to suggest that Stella stay back and miss all this fun.

She probably didn't know who Old MacDonald was, but once she saw him, she would know.

And Project Pericarp would be clearer to all.

Also clearer would be who Ulysses was to the FBI and other government entities who would love to get their hands on his brain.

It was too bad that Aspasia had disappeared again after that meeting with Cayson at the data storage convention.

Cayson was confident that the woman who

activated his implants was Aspasia. Elusive. Evil.
And madly in love with Ulysses.

They took a five-minute break in a clearing.

Slap!

"Aarrgghh!" Stella growled as she slapped her
cheek and scratched. "I'm wearing long pants and a
long-sleeved shirt, and the mosquitoes went for my
face."

There were red welts all over her face.

"Your slap was probably worse than their bites,"
Cayson said.

"Are you kidding me now?" Stella glared at
him. "Why aren't they biting you?"

"You're sweet, that's why." Cayson laughed.
"Those southern mosquitoes love you."

"Remind me why I shouldn't move to Georgia,"
Stella said, wincing and massaging her arm around
her stitches. "How much longer do we have?"

Cayson didn't know. They turned to Tyrone,
who seemed to refuse to answer them.

"You don't have to tell us." Cayson waved at
him. "If there were a zip line, we'd get to him in no
time, right?"

They resumed their trek as the late afternoon
sun peeked in every now and then when there was
a break in the forest canopy.

Here in the forest, Cayson felt cut off from the

outside world. He wondered about new developments at VenomLabs.

Are they going to fire someone for the breach of security?

Who is Mole Rat?

Had VenomLabs done any direct business with Molyneux? Cayson wouldn't put it past the contractor to be competitive against other DOD contractors.

He wouldn't put it past VenomLabs to do something to stir up trouble so that the DOD would do massive orders of this or that.

Who knows.

Cayson prayed quietly for his cousin, Leland, that she would be okay. Whenever she had to fly to Europe for projects for the CIA or FBI, Leland was often incommunicado. Now it was his turn to be away.

All Cayson could do was ask God to keep them all safe.

T he welcome party at Still Waters Farm included a three-legged sheepdog, one Great Dane, three cats, a cow who skipped around, and five goats. They were inside a second fence away from the dirt road.

All roamed freely under God's open skies and rolling green fields that stretched to the edge of the forest.

"The chickens are somewhere." Tyrone got off his dirt-encrusted bicycle and removed his helmet. Part of his face was dusty and grimy.

Her arm in great pain, Stella leaned against the fence as they waited for someone to open the gate for them. She shouldn't have come.

Tyrone got off his phone, which worked in the open field.

That told Stella that they were probably near a town or a cell tower near a town.

That phone bothered Stella. Could anyone find them here? All they had to do was triangulate...

A small truck rumbled through the farm toward them on the winding dirt road.

This was the first truck Stella had seen in the area. A second clue that they were near town.

If so, why did they have to hike through the forest? Why couldn't they have driven around the entire forest to get here?

Its windows were down, and some instrumental jazz was playing from the dashboard. It came to a stop a yard away from the gate.

When Stella saw who came out of the truck, it became all clear to her.

Could that be who they all called Old MacDonald?

To Stella, he was Dmitri Proskouriakoff, only one of Russia's best old-school hackers. Highly sought after by the CIA, he had given up his motherland citizenship to move to the United States to train NSA hackers on how to destroy FSB systems.

Some people, including Stella, had wondered if Dmitri's heart was still Russian.

And whether he still worked for the FSB.

Dmitri eyed her as he unlocked the gate. He did not recognize her.

Well, *he* was easy on the eyes, in spite of his age. From Stella's recollection, Dmitri was in his seventies. He looked fit. He looked like he could take her down.

Hadn't Tyrone said that he was a drone expert?

Who owned the armed drones in the forest? They had a few samples strapped to their bicycles, but what if those drones belonged to Dmitri?

Dmitri greeted Tyrone first, like they were best buddies. Then he turned his attention to Cayson.

"I haven't seen you in forever." Dmitri shook Cayson's hand.

"I thought you moved home to Russia."

Dmitri shrugged. "I can't leave my farm. Just bought another twenty baby chicks."

One of FSB's best hackers was raising chickens in America. Stella couldn't wrap her mind around it.

"And who is this?" Dmitri bowed to Stella.

"Stella Evans, a friend of Cayson's." She shook his hand.

"Just a friend?" He looked disappointed.

CHAPTER EIGHTEEN

"Vegetables and herbs from my garden." Dmitri beamed with pride at the spread he had offered his guests at dinner. "I planted, I watered, but God gave me the harvest."

Sitting adjacent to Cayson, Stella waited for him to say something about thanking God for the food. She didn't know Dmitri from Adam and wasn't sure if he was a praying man.

He had mentioned God though.

Cayson squeezed Stella's hand. "Shall we say a blessing?"

Stella nodded slightly. And so Cayson did. Afterward, the loudest *amen* came from Dmitri.

Stella tasted her salad. "Mmm. Very good."

"Told you," Dmitri said. "You cannot outplant or outgrow God."

"You say 'God' a lot," Cayson said. "In the past, you didn't talk about God much. You weren't religious at all."

"Five heart attacks can change a man." Dmitri dabbed the corners of his lips with a cloth napkin.

"What? You? You look too healthy..."

Dmitri raised his hand. "Let me rephrase that. I did not get five heart attacks. Ulysses did. His suffering changed me. Or shall I say, I got scared."

Ulysses.

"Speaking of him, where is he?" Stella asked.

Dmitri didn't answer her.

"You used to cuss a mile a minute," Cayson said to Dmitri, cutting off Stella's inquiry.

She was sure the men had heard her question. She was miffed at Cayson for not following her lead here.

Didn't he realize what was at stake?

Didn't he want to know where Ulysses went?

They were not just having lunch with an old friend. They had to find a way to get back to Atlanta, extract Icarus from Cayson's head, shut down MedusaNet, and do all that without getting killed.

"Ah, I keep my mouth clean these days," Dmitri said. "Good for the soul."

"Is it?" Stella asked.

"Is it not?" Dmitri replied.

Stella could say a number of things in response, but something in her spirit told her to stand down.

And wait.

There's a time to speak and a time to listen.

"Well, you cussed in Russian," Cayson said. "I'm sure most of it was lost in translation."

Dmitri laughed.

It was an interesting laugh, Stella thought. Kind of a cross between contentment and chaos.

Contentment because Dmitri seemed happy, albeit living by himself in a rustic log cabin in the middle of nowhere in this mosquito-infested deep south.

Chaos because surrounding this retreat of his were swarms of drones protecting his property and his life.

That told Stella one thing: Dmitri had enemies.

Dmitri had called the drones his civilized air patrol.

Civilized.

Stella smiled as she recalled Dmitri mentioning that he had named his drones Sheepdogs.

He hadn't said how many there were.

"You're FBI," Dmitri said.

"This is my last assignment," Stella replied.

"Was."

Finishing up her salad, Stella thought about that single word Dmitri had said about her last assignment.

Was.

This was *my last assignment.*

This is *my last assignment.*

What in the world did Dmitri mean by changing the tense of her sentence? Was she heading to a new assignment? What did Dmitri know about it? How?

"I have another question," Stella said.

"Yes?"

"Since this is a farm, wouldn't you have access to a main road of some sort that could take you to town?"

Dmitri nodded. "Yes, we do. But you have to drive four hours around the forest to get there."

"Better than hiking all day and nearly getting killed."

"Going through Tyrone to get to Dmitri is a test," Dmitri explained. "However, neither of us sent those drones. We usually leave you to the natural elements in the forest. You survive, you survive. You die, you die."

"How compassionate."

"Most people give up." Dmitri threw his hands up.

"We didn't."

"Exactly."

"So you're saying you could drive to Dahlonega from here instead of having to hike through the forest," Stella said.

"Yes, but it wasn't always the case—until a neighbor sold their land to the DOT and they built a road through that piece of land, giving us access to the outside world."

"Now you benefit," Stella said.

"I had no idea," Cayson said.

"They built it after Leland came to visit," Dmitri explained.

When Dmitri's personal chef brought out prettily plated catfish for their lunch, Cayson rubbed his palms together and dug in so quickly that Stella realized she hadn't known that part about Cayson.

His profile had been on the FBI records for her to see.

Born in Florida and raised in Georgia because his father had found a new job teaching at the Georgia Institute of Technology—better known as Georgia Tech—Cayson had grown up in a technology-driven home. His mother was an intellectual property attorney for some big software companies.

Cayson's favorite color was green, and he hated driving in Atlanta traffic.

But nowhere in his profile did it say he liked catfish.

Stella was so deep in thought that she didn't realize Dmitri was looking at her. Waiting for something?

She broke a piece of the catfish with her fork and put it in her mouth. It was breaded.

"Panko breadcrumbs," Dmitri said.

Oh, he had been waiting for her assessment of the dish.

Stella was more curious about the fact that Dmitri had a personal chef but lived in a log cabin that looked so old and rustic that nobody would tell he was anything but poor.

Then again, poverty is in the mind, is it not?

"Very good." Stella ate more.

Dmitri smiled. Satisfied. "To answer your earlier question, Ulysses has left the country. He didn't say where he was going or whether he will ever return. He doesn't like your government, and he wants to find a better place to live. The last time I heard from him, he was traveling through India."

Oh. "America is not for everyone."

"Especially not for Ulysses," Cayson said. "Why did you ask about him?"

"The woman at the convention was trying to contact Ulysses," Stella said.

"I hope they find her before she returns to Macau."

Stella didn't correct Cayson. The woman who had called herself Aspasia wasn't from Macau. Jake Kessler was searching for her.

Jake Kessler.

Stella hoped that Kessler wasn't in any danger. Isolated from her work, Stella had no idea what was going on out there. All she knew was that there were many unanswered questions.

The events had piled up in her mind.

How had their attackers found them at the gas station down the road from VenomLabs?

Why had Kessler told her not to trust anyone— not even himself? Had the FBI intranet been compromised? By whom?

Should she try to contact Kessler?

"...Aspasia."

The trigger word snapped Stella out of her jumbled thoughts.

"Why would she ask about Ulysses?" Dmitri asked. "She should know that Ulysses doesn't want to be found. Even I don't know where he is."

"Unless she wasn't Aspasia after all," Cayson said. "Although, I must say, she looked like Aspasia."

"Plastic surgery can do wonders these days," Dmitri suggested. He opened his mouth to say more, but he stopped.

Cayson put his hand on Stella's shoulder. "You can trust her."

"I trust no one." Dmitri stared at Stella. "I don't even trust myself."

"Then who can we trust?"

"God, of course," Stella said.

"Of course."

Even though Dmitri said no more, Stella felt she had cracked the glass wall between her and the old hacker. Perhaps down the road she could call him if they needed—

No.

This is my last assignment, remember?

CHAPTER NINETEEN

"I know what you're thinking." Dmitri pointed to Cayson. "I'm wasting my talent."

Cayson didn't say anything. In fact, he had been thinking that he should offer Dmitri a full-time hacking job at Binary Systems.

"I'm not, I tell you. I'm finally enjoying life." Sitting under the evening stars on his back porch, Dmitri looked pensive. "I'm too old for new adventures, friend."

Cayson nodded. "It's stressful."

Like what he had been feeling these several weeks with Icarus in his head.

Sitting on the other side of Cayson, Stella

didn't say anything. Cayson wondered what she was thinking.

"The stress was killing me," Dmitri explained. "When Ulysses had those heart attacks, I knew I'd be next to get some life-changing disease, or I could walk out."

"So you changed your scenery," Cayson said.

"Yep. Just like that. I feel healthier."

"What are you saying? You're not going to help us?" Cayson didn't know how else to phrase it.

"I'm retired. I don't want to be involved." Dmitri leaned toward Cayson. "I don't need another medal from the FSB. They might call me to more work. Then who's going to take care of my goats? My cows?"

Cayson wondered whether to let him just keep talking.

Obviously, Dmitri was trying to rationalize why he should not help the United States government and its various entities, notably DARPA and the NSA in this particular go-round.

"Let me show you something, Dmitri." Cayson looked around. "We may have to go inside."

Stella and Dmitri followed him into the log cabin. Cayson pulled the window curtains closed. Then he asked someone to turn off the light. Dmitri did.

Cayson stood in front of Dmitri. "Icarus, flashlight."

And Cayson's head glowed green again.

Dmitri flinched.

"So they did it," he finally said.

"I beg you to please undo it. They implanted Icarus in my head against my will. I never consented to it. I was unconscious."

Dmitri said nothing for a long time. "I haven't hacked in ages."

"It's like riding a bicycle, et cetera."

"How is Leland these days?"

"She is doing great. You taught her well. Best of her class."

Dmitri shrugged. "There are many other old-school hackers who could have taught her."

"But there's only one you." Cayson sighed. "She has been trying. Three hackers have been assassinated. One more has disappeared. It's just Leland and me. Another NSA contractor wants to help, but they're not ready. We need you."

When Dmitri said nothing, Cayson added, "This implant is killing me."

"We can't do it here. I don't have enough bandwidth. I need some tools, and they're in Moscow. If I ask for them now, the tools will be here in one or two days."

"Thank you! Thank you!" Cayson blurted, restraining himself from getting too excited. He didn't want to confuse Icarus and cause himself any harm.

Harm?

How ironic it was that just days ago, he had jumped off the cliff of Trolltunga.

"Wait a second." Stella raised her hand. "Did you say Moscow?"

Dmitri nodded. "But you will owe the FSB. And they will collect. They never forget."

Morning came into Cayson's bedroom through the rectangular windows like there wasn't a single care in the whole wide world. He had left the curtains pulled back the night before so he could see the stars in the sky.

Now the sun had awoken him too early.

All Cayson wanted to do was stay wrapped in this warm wool blanket and go back to sleep.

But sleep didn't resume.

He heard dogs barking and people laughing outside, on the grounds somewhere.

He rolled out of bed and shuffled to the

window, dragging the blanket around his shoulders. The September weather was cool, not chilly, but he would've preferred much warmer weather than this.

Outside and one floor down, he spotted Dmitri and his cane, Stella with her hands in her pockets, a dog, a goat, and several ducks.

Ducks?

I didn't know Dmitri had ducks.

The animals were milling about the two people, who were talking away. It was nice to see Dmitri warming up to Stella, but Cayson was sure that at the back of Dmitri's mind, he hadn't forgotten that Stella had a badge.

For the moment, they seemed like two amicable people chatting in...

Russian?

He could hear them through the thin windows.

Cayson didn't know that Stella spoke Russian.

"Icarus, profile Stella Evans." Cayson surprised himself.

"No internet connection."

Ah. A lockdown.

This was how Dmitri stayed safe in the woods. He was simply off the grid.

What about the phone call that Tyrone made to Dmitri? Someone else's phone, perhaps?

It had been several years since he had seen Dmitri, but they had resumed their friendship as though there had been no break since their last project together.

Cayson tried to recall his own feelings when Leland had mentioned Old MacDonald to him back in the rubble of the VenomLabs machine room.

He hadn't expected to have to run to Old MacDonald this soon. They had agreed to not call on him unless it was an emergency.

Does the penalty of death count as an emergency?

Dmitri hadn't made it hard for Cayson to find him. It was apparent to Cayson now that Dmitri had been involved in their rescue from the armed drones in the forest.

How else would Tyrone's squad have been successful in shooting down the drones?

And why would Tyrone let the teenagers salvage the drones for parts? He must've known they had destroyed the drones thoroughly.

Dmitri had been in contact with Tyrone, hadn't he?

Perhaps he had even known that Cayson and Stella had been on their way. No wonder Dmitri hadn't looked surprised when he met them at his farm gate.

Cayson was still standing at the window when Dmitri looked his way from where he was at the edge of the manicured lawn. Stella was looking away into the distance.

Dmitri waved.

Cayson waved back.

He wondered whether Dmitri had been in contact with Leland.

He probably has.

If so, how much did Dmitri know about MedusaNet?

"What time is it?" Cayson looked around the room. There was not a single clock anywhere. "Icarus, time?"

7:26 AM.

"Wow. I could get used to a personal assistant," Cayson mumbled.

If only he wasn't stuck to my brain.

CHAPTER TWENTY

S tella was the first person to reach the dining room for breakfast. Her hair was still damp from the shower, and she didn't feel like going back to her room to use the hair dryer again. She figured that her hair would dry soon enough.

Cayson was probably getting ready. She had seen his shadow at the window, waving to Dmitri. She would have waved back had she not been deep in thought about what Dmitri had told her about the FSB and their operations in North America. By the time she lifted her head toward the second-floor window, all she could see was Cayson moving away from the window.

That hadn't been important to Stella. On her walk with Dmitri across the grass, she had heard something in the wind, but it had turned out to be only the wind.

Sometimes the great outdoors brought with it strange sounds.

Still, Stella couldn't help but imagine that the distant sounds—noises—she had heard were yet more of Dmitri's drones.

In some ways, it had been a waste for Dmitri to retire his ingenuity.

Then again, he might not have retired after all.

Stella heard muffled noises coming from the kitchen and decided to investigate. As soon as she reached the kitchen door, the housekeeper greeted her.

"Good morning." Mirabella remained standing where she was, leaning against the ceramic farmhouse kitchen counter and texting on her phone.

On the island in front of her, a countertop-mounted robot arm broke another egg onto a frying pan. Another arm with a scanner scanned the other eggs in the pan and then flipped them.

"Morning." Stella stared at the mechanical cook.

"You want yours scrambled, right?" Mirabella asked.

She had taken orders the night before and no doubt had programmed the robot cook.

Stella nodded. "Wow."

Mirabella put down her phone. "I'm surprised that you're surprised."

"Well..." Stella stepped closer to the island. "What else does it cook?"

"Hamburgers, fried rice, and pretty much anything you want on a griddle."

"Like on a hibachi grill?"

Mirabella nodded. "Frankly, I don't know why Dmitri hired me. I can barely cook. If not for M2371—Max—over here, we'd have burnt toast for breakfast every morning."

So what do you do? Stella was glad her thoughts didn't pop out of her mouth.

"If Dmitri bought or invented robots to do the laundry and clean the bathrooms, I'd be out of a job."

"I hate cleaning bathrooms," Stella said.

"Me too." Mirabella pointed to the coffeemaker. "Want some coffee?"

"Sure."

"This I can handle." Mirabella laughed as she picked a mug from the mug stand next to the coffeemaker.

There was nothing unusual about the house-keeper. Stella pegged her to be in her late twenties or early thirties.

At this time, Mirabella didn't seem suspicious.

Then again, Stella was in a gray area now, that no man's land where she couldn't be sure if she still had a job when she returned to the FBI whenever they made it home. Being chased like a fugitive had left a bad taste in her mouth and made her feel as if her last ten years of serving her country had been in vain.

She had decided to quit, hadn't she?

Perhaps they had decided to fire her after all.

She couldn't name an assignment in which there had been an internal investigation on her. But these last couple of years after the end of Project Pericarp had been nothing but messy.

The only good thing that had come out of it was Cayson Yang.

They had kept in sporadic touch with each other after that operation, though the residue had followed them to this day and had left three Binary Systems employees dead.

If she could help it, Cayson would not die.

Then again, was it up to her?

"So you like your job as a federal agent?" Mirabella handed Stella a steamy cup of coffee. She did not ask Stella if she wanted cream and sugar.

How did Mirabella know that Stella drank her coffee black?

"Dmitri said Cayson told him that you drink your coffee bitter," Mirabella offered, as if guessing what had been in Stella's mind.

"Ah, all the important details." Stella wondered why no one else had come down for breakfast yet.

Speaking of which...

Stella turned to find four plates of eggs and sausages lined up on the countertop.

Mirabella glanced at her phone. "Dmitri will be here any minute now."

Stella still couldn't read her.

When curious, ask nonthreatening questions. "What would you do if you weren't working here?"

Mirabella seemed to think about it for a minute. "I'd travel the world, I suppose."

"That sounds fun."

"Your voice doesn't say you think it's fun," Mirabella replied. "But for me, having been cooped up in this isolated farm for several years, it would be a change of scenery for me."

"Why didn't you leave?" Stella sipped hot coffee, feeling pain in her arm. She probably needed to see a doctor. Get a tetanus shot or something.

"I feel sorry for Dmitri," Mirabella said.

"He looks like a nice gentleman."

"He is." Mirabella's voice was quiet.

"So if you had a chance to travel the world, where would you go first?"

Mirabella shrugged. "Anywhere people don't know me, but it has to be someplace with Wi-Fi."

"Of course."

~

Halfway through breakfast, Stella's arm throbbed something fierce. Her stitches burned, and she could barely hold the fork in her hand.

She turned to Dmitri, sitting across the table—drinking water and staring at her.

"Do you have any painkillers?" Stella asked.

Dmitri put his goblet down on the table. "Let's have a look."

Stella winced as she gingerly pulled up her sleeves to reveal angry flesh around the stitches.

Cayson cleared his throat. "Can't we look at that after breakfast?"

Dmitri ignored him. "You probably need a doctor to look at it."

What was he implying?

"Tyrone's community... They can't treat a

common cold, let alone..." Dmitri waved his arms about.

"I didn't think anyone could treat a common cold." Cayson stretched his hand toward Stella. "You okay?"

"I don't want to say it hurts, but it does." Stella could feel the taut inflammation on her arm. She wondered what sort of infection she now had. And how long it would last.

"I know a doctor in town," Dmitri said. "He won't tell anyone you're here."

"What sort of doctor?" Stella asked.

Next to Dmitri, Mirabella lifted her goblet. "Large animals."

Stella nearly choked on her own saliva. "As in, a vet?"

"Is that what they're called?" Dmitri deadpanned.

This was not going well. "What about downtown Dahlonega?"

"They're going to report a gunshot wound."

"It's just a flesh wound." Stella prayed that was all there was to it. "Grazed my arm and went right through it."

"So why aren't you better now?"

"Maybe the forest doesn't suit me."

Cayson looked up to the ceiling. "Icarus, what sort of germs are in the forest?"

Stella waited as Cayson nodded. He recited aloud what Icarus told him in his head, numerous scientific names, including all variations of coliform.

"Stop it," Stella said. "I don't want to hear any more."

But she knew then that she couldn't go with them back to Atlanta.

"We'll get some help in Atlanta," Cayson said.

"Nothing for me to do there," Stella countered. "I'm not a hacker."

"You kept me alive in Marietta."

"God did."

"Through you." Cayson swallowed. "I wouldn't have survived."

"You guys go to Atlanta. I'll stay here with Mirabella."

"I've got errands to run in town, but I'll be back shortly," Mirabella said.

Stella nodded. "I'll be fine here with the cats and goats. I just need to rest."

She felt warm all over her body. Her system was probably fighting off something. Being non-medical had its drawbacks. She had no idea what was happening to her.

Her thoughts went back to when she was eight years old, falling off the chicken coop in her parents' backyard. How she had gotten up to the roof of the coop was another story, but once she was up there, the next problem was how to get down.

She hadn't anticipated her canvas shoes slipping on the zinc roof.

Seven stitches on her left leg later, she had learned her lesson—that was, she hated the doctor's office.

Yeah, after twenty-three years and many more falls, stitches, and broken bones, she knew that had been the wrong lesson.

"Let's pray for you." Cayson reached for Stella's good hand.

They bowed their heads. Cayson said a quick but heartfelt prayer that God would heal Stella's wounds.

"And God of the universe, we pray this in the strong name of Jesus. Amen."

Dmitri's *amen* was particularly loud.

Silently, Stella added her own prayers for the two men's safety as they traveled back to Atlanta. Her mind was too foggy to think of anything else requiring God's help at this time. She was sure there were many dangers they all needed protection from, but all she wanted to do now was rest.

Sleep. Get well.

Cayson started clearing the table. "May I take your plate?"

When Stella looked down, she realized her plate was completely empty. She didn't remember eating any of her breakfast.

"Looks like you liked your toast and scrambled eggs with cheese," Cayson said.

I had toast?

"I think I'll go lie down," she said.

Dmitri pointed to the sunroom across the hall from the dining room. "The couch there is very comfortable. You also have a view of the sky."

Stella nodded.

"Mirabella will be here if you need anything," Dmitri added.

Stella nodded again.

CHAPTER TWENTY-ONE

Moscow Mechanics was a misnomer. The establishment in downtown Decatur, Georgia, was not an auto repair shop nor did anyone from Russia work there. In fact, it was run by a Taiwanese businessman from Vancouver who loved Bollywood musicals and Italian opera.

In the sparsely furnished lobby, Cayson watched the tearful reunion between his cousin Leland and her mentor, Dmitri. But the hugs were short lived. They had little time to spare for a cup of tea, and everyone knew it.

Still, Cayson wished he had gotten a proper hug from Leland.

Isn't she happy to see her favorite cousin?

On the main floor of the office complex, Dmitri and Leland led Cayson through a maze of cluttered workstations to a back hallway where an old elevator opened its doors to welcome the dead—

"Oh sorry." Cayson grimaced.

Leland was tapping and swiping her tablet computer, ignoring him.

"Huh?" Dmitri didn't seem to be aware of his thoughts.

Of course.

Not even Icarus was privy to Cayson's thoughts. Unless he expressed them in words, Icarus could not read his mind.

Only God could read his mind.

"I didn't mean to be grim," Cayson said.

"About what?" Dmitri pushed the elevator button.

"Being grim. I mean—well, yes, I meant it. We're all already dead."

Dmitri said nothing.

"Never mind."

Dmitri invited him to enter the elevator first. Stepping in, Dmitri pushed a button.

Cayson's eyes blurred. He winced. Which button was that?

"Are we going up to heaven?" Cayson leaned against the steel wall.

"We'd better get Icarus out of your head before your gibberish turns into a sonnet or something."

To which Cayson began to hum.

"You were fine yesterday," Dmitri added.

"And this morning. Is it still day?"

"I could slap you upside the head," Dmitri offered. "That could either reboot Icarus or...kill you."

"How shall I choose?" Cayson's hands began to shake. "Why are my hands shaking?"

"Fear of death, perhaps?" Leland suggested.

Cayson clenched his fists. "Why is this elevator so slow?"

"Would you rather it free-fall?" Dmitri asked.

Cayson felt dizzy.

Dmitri reached for him. "Relax, friend. It's not the end of the world."

"But it could be the end of me."

"And another will take your place."

"Not helping!" Cayson waved him off. He moaned again.

"Motion sickness?" Dmitri asked.

"Why is this elevator so slow?" Cayson slid down to the floor. "How far do we have to go? Such things I do not know."

Dmitri chuckled. "Wow. I didn't know Icarus was a poet."

"Icarus?"

The elevator door opened.

Mole Rat.

Cayson sprang to his feet, wobbled a bit, and grabbed Dmitri's arm. "He just called me Mole Rat. Or did he?"

Dmitri didn't respond.

"Did you hear me?" Cayson didn't care if he sounded desperate.

Dmitri put a finger on his lips.

Cayson nodded.

Dmitri led him down a brightly lit hallway. He walked slowly, as if by walking any faster, he would alert the duality of Icarus.

Duality?

In a moment of lucidity, Cayson frowned.

Perhaps Icarus was talking to someone else named Mole Rat. It was impossible for him to be Mole Rat. They had established that Mole Rat was in the employ of Molyneux.

Dmitri glanced at Cayson. Nodded.

Cayson nodded back, though he had zero idea why Dmitri had nodded at him.

"Icarus, what is my name?" Cayson suddenly asked.

Chameleon.

"Icarus is going bonkers," Cayson concluded.

He thought about his recent stay at VenomLabs on the other side of metro Atlanta in the city of Marietta.

What could Reyes have possibly done to him while he had been under the knife?

Had they done what had been in his interest?

Or had VenomLabs tweaked his implants? Perhaps they had added software into the Icarus unit?

Could that have been how the armed drones had found them in the forest outside Dahlonega?

If that had been the case, by his presence, Cayson had endangered an entire off-the-grid community of people minding their own business, plus Dmitri and his housekeeper and—

Stella.

We have to warn her!

CHAPTER TWENTY-TWO

S tella hadn't heard a thing. Not a door opening, not footsteps. Nothing.

She had been taking a nap in the living room.

The housekeeper had gone shopping for food.

The dogs and cats came and went. But they were polite and respectfully quiet.

Stella smelled him first. A combination of pot and alcohol.

When she opened her eyes, she saw a Colt in his hand. She had to assume it was loaded since it was pointed at her. She had seen too many people pointing weapons at her lately.

But this was a new one.

Osman Reyes of the famed VenomLabs.

A scientist with a PhD in robotics from the Massachusetts Institute of Technology.

And now what? A traitor extraordinaire?

"Dr. Reyes, what brings you to town?" Stella spoke calmly, regretting that she had left her Glock... Where?

She could not feel her Glock anywhere on her person. Her waist holster felt empty.

She tried to move. Her head spun.

Whoa. Why am I feeling groggy?

All she had done was take a nap.

Now she felt as though she had been drugged.

Reyes didn't seem to care what she felt.

He waved that Colt in her face. "Dmitri has some papers that belong to me."

"Papers?" Stella hid her surprise that Reyes had asked for paper. "Digital paper?"

"Real paper. Dmitri is old school."

"He wrote something down with a pen?" *I don't have it. Dmitri didn't say...* "Are you sure it's here?"

"Don't mess with me."

It was then that Stella saw a trickle of liquid coming out his nose. Thick and dark.

Reyes wiped it on the back of his hand. Stared at the red smear. His hand started to shake.

"Let me give you one word: evidence." Angry voice. "I must have it."

"Let me give you another word: treason."

Before Reyes could respond, Stella's Krava Maga kicked in. She knocked the Colt out of Reyes's hand, went for his vital organs, threw him onto the couch, and pinned him there.

To kill him.

Or be killed.

She knew she had popped out at least one stitch on her arm.

The pain seared.

But Reyes wasn't finished. He flailed his arms, nails scratching Stella.

Before she could restrain Reyes's arms, blood began to ooze out of his eyes and ears. He screamed.

His eyes rolled back, and his entire head exploded, splattering warm brain matter, fluid, and blood all over Stella, just as the only phone in the farmhouse rang.

"It's Osman Reyes," Cayson said on the speakerphone.

"Yeah, I know." Stella kept wiping her face with a clean kitchen towel she had found.

The police were on their way. When the phone had rung, Stella had picked it up, but she had put Cayson on hold while she called 911.

"And you know that—how?" Cayson asked.

"He was here." Stella wiped gunk and blood off her arms. "He still is, but let's just say he's non-responsive."

"You knocked him out?" Cayson's voice suddenly turned shrill. "We called you too late! I wish you had come with us. If anything had happened to you—"

"Nothing happened to me." Nothing too serious, anyway. Two busted stitches. A ruined borrowed shirt. That sort of thing.

"Thank God."

"Yes, He protected me and kept me safe." Stella was glad the phone was an old model and didn't have video.

If Cayson had seen her with her bloodied blouse, he'd probably freak out.

And why did she care?

I do care.

"Dmitri wants to talk to you," Cayson said.

Stella waited until she heard Dmitri. He was wheezing.

"Has Mirabella returned?" he asked.

"No. She's gone to the grocery store." Stella wondered if the thirty-something-year-old housekeeper was more than that to Dmitri.

"She's not answering her phone."

"Do you want me to go look for her?" Stella asked.

"Do you know where the grocery store is?"

"She told me before she left. The local PD is on their way. I'll talk to them about Mirabella."

"No." A pause. Then: "Miss Evans?"

"Stella."

"Stella, I need you to find Mirabella and take her to a safe house. There's a tunnel in the kitchen that leads to the forest. Outside the opening, there's a shed nearby with two bicycles inside."

"I don't know this area—"

"My drones will help you find the safe house."

"Why didn't they track down Mirabella?"

"I don't know. I hope she didn't turn them off."

"Why would she..." A thousand things percolated in Stella's mind. "Tell me Mirabella is not a cyborg."

Dmitri laughed. "No, no. She's my daughter, but she doesn't know that. Don't tell her."

"Ah, I don't need to get into domestic squabbles."

"Her mother and I... She died because of me."

"And you don't want your daughter to know."

His voice hardened. "Maria was a spy. She used me!"

"You said she's dead. Let the dead rest, Dmitri."

"What? You're counseling me now?" Dmitri snapped.

The doorbell rang.

"I think the local PD is here." Stella turned. "I'll ask them to help me find Mirabella."

Silence. Then: "Stella, do not open the door."

"It's not the police, is it?"

"It's Aspasia and her men."

"Still looking for Ulysses, is she?" Stella backtracked toward the back of the house even though she suspected the entire farm was likely surrounded.

"She probably thinks Ulysses is me," Dmitri said. "Go to the kitchen and into the cellar. In the cellar is a door to a tunnel. The tunnel comes out on the other side of the farm. I will ask Tyrone to meet you there."

The doorbell rang again.

"Go, Stella—"

An explosion rocked the house.

Stella ran for her life through the hallway lined with a blur of paintings and mirrors, entering the small farmhouse kitchen where pots, pans, and broken plates had scattered all over the floor from the explosion.

Among cracks on the walls, a pantry door gaped at her, ripped open at the hinges.

"Where is the cellar?" Stella asked, but the phone was silent.

The entire house was bathed in silence.

She wasn't sure what that explosion had been, but since her phone had stopped working, she guessed that Aspasia had deployed some sort of localized e-bomb. Low-level electromagnetic pulses had probably taken out the electronics in this house.

EMP again.

Not that Reyes hadn't already disabled the security system prior to the arrival of the new enemies.

She heard the distinct shuffling of feet and the

sounds of metal rubbing against heavy armor, and knew she was running out of time.

God, I need You now!

Where is the cellar?

Her eyes swept the kitchen in the afternoon sunlight coming through a couple of rectangular windows.

Instinctively, she reached for her holster again.

Empty.

Where is the cellar?

Click.

She spun around. Part of a wall moved. An arm popped out and waved to her.

"In here!" Mirabella opened the door wider.

Stella made a dash for it, and Mirabella shut the door just as a barrage of gunfire hit the door on the other side.

"Is this the cellar?" Stella asked, out of breath.

"Well, yeah. Dmitri calls it whatever he wants."

It was a small space, hardly standing height. Stella's five-eight frame bent over, and she could feel the strain in her spine as she ran through the tunnel, with Mirabella leading the way.

She held a flashlight in front of her. "The electricity is not working. EMP, probably."

She knows.

"When did you get back?" Stella asked.

"Minutes ago. The drones were offline. I figured something was wrong." Mirabella frowned. "The bad news is that Dmitri's favorite ice cream is in the van."

Does she know who Dmitri really is to her?

"He tried to contact you." Stella paused to catch her breath. Her arm hurt. Even in the dim light, she could see that it was bleeding around her stitches.

"I figured."

"If this is the tunnel he spoke of, then Tyrone is waiting for us at the other end."

Mirabella nodded. "I know. We've rehearsed this."

"Then why did Dmitri tell me to take *you* to this tunnel?"

"He worries about me a lot."

"Why do you think?" As soon as the question left her lips, Stella realized this was simply the wrong time to talk about life-changing family matters.

Mirabella stopped at the end of the tunnel, where a rung ladder, rusty in places, went straight up toward a circular door.

She turned toward Stella. "Because fathers worry about their daughters."

"So you know."

"I've known since the week after he hired me to cook for him and manage his drones."

"Ah, in that order."

"A man's got to eat." Mirabella laughed. "He's actually a good cook himself. He doesn't need me. I'm only here because I remind him of Mother."

"You knew her before she died?"

"I also know who killed her, but I can't tell Dmitri." Mirabella put one boot on the bottom rung of the ladder. She looked up. "Come on, Tyrone. Open the door!"

Distant noises from the ground above them startled both of them. The tremor dislodged bits of earth and dirt, sprinkling debris over them.

"Stand back!" Mirabella leapt off the bottom rung of the ladder.

The two women took cover as the hatch lifted at the top of the ladder. Shadowy daylight streamed into the tunnel.

"Mirabella!" It was Tyrone's voice. "Let's go."

CHAPTER TWENTY-THREE

Osman Reyes's real name was indeed Osman Reyes. Three PhDs, two professorships, five patents pending—and he was still as dead as a headless doornail.

His accolades didn't matter as much as the fact that he had been one of a dozen VenomLabs employees who had been compromised by Molyneux in a project that had far-reaching consequences too numerous to count.

"Best to leave it to the Feds," Cayson said aloud.

He glanced around the Moscow Mechanics computer room and realized that Stella Evans wasn't there.

With me.

Dmitri's Atlanta associates had taken Stella to a twenty-four-hour private clinic to have her arm looked at. She should be back soon.

Cayson wished they had more time to spend together in a non-working environment. It had been three years since he knew Stella, and they still hadn't had any downtime.

At some point in the last three years, Stella had mentioned that she had been trying to leave the FBI.

Where would she go?

What would she do?

Cayson wanted her by his side...

For life.

A waving hand in front of his eyes broke his muse.

"Stop daydreaming, cuz." Leland shook her head. "Stella is going to be fine."

"How do you know what I was thinking?"

Leland shrugged. "We've been cousins since I was born. I know when you're worried."

"I'm not *worried* worried."

"My only concern is that they took Stella to a private clinic. All medical records are logged." Leland walked back to her workstation two chairs away.

Her statement gave Cayson pause.

He wanted to ask Leland if something could be done, but his eyes spotted Raj Subramaniam watching him a few workstations away from Leland's.

Raj wasn't a tall or big man, but his billion-dollar presence in the Moscow Mechanics machine room spoke volumes.

When they had arrived the day before, Cayson had been surprised to find out that Dmitri had originally owned this cybernetics laboratory. He had sold fifty-one percent of it to his Taiwanese business partner.

Less than twenty-four hours ago, both Cayson and Dmitri had found out that Mr. Bao had sold his majority share to Raj Subramaniam, CEO of a cyber security company that frequently carried out classified assignments for the United States and other world governments.

And here he was.

Raj Subramaniam himself. Listed in *Forbes* as one of a handful of multibillionaires under forty, Raj was a product of Bangalore, India, where his family still resided. His IQ was off the charts and in the clouds, and less than an hour ago, he had proposed a merger with Binary Systems.

Seriously.

Leland had answered for both of them with a resounding *no*.

As in, "We want to remain dirt poor. Thank you very much."

Cayson thought he should try to change his business partner's mind soon, but the fact that she was also his cousin now became an obstacle for him.

He'd have to think about it later, as a set of double doors opened and in ambled Dmitri, accompanied by a bevy of men and women in waiting.

"You ready for the interface, Cayson, my boy?"

Instead of answering Dmitri, Cayson searched the group. "Where's Stella?"

"Reassigned," Dmitri replied.

"What? Where?" Cayson's fingers gripped the armrest. "Wait a sec. How did they know she was here?"

"Everything will be answered soon. Right now, let's get you plugged in." Dmitri motioned for Cayson to go with him.

"I'm not moving until I know what's going on."

"Pouting, I see." Dmitri shook his head. "If you must know, Stella is with Jake Kessler. You remember him from NCIJTF? They're going to take down the FBI field office in Chamblee."

"So there was a mole after all."

Mole Rat.

And Cayson knew now that Icarus hadn't been referring to him.

CHAPTER TWENTY-FOUR

Cayson had half-expected the private laboratory to be brightly lit like a winter wonderland with snow drifts—

What?

Cayson blinked.

The room was cavernous and painted white, yes, but it was stark and smelled of doom and defeat.

Only, Cayson wasn't sure if the defeat was on his side or Molyneux's side.

He looked around for a hospital bed, praying that they would put him under so he wouldn't feel the crawl of tentacles under his scalp.

No offense, Icarus.

Icarus didn't respond.

Two lab technicians led him to a changing room, which turned out to be a sterilization chamber meant to scrape every layer of dead skin off of him and clean his entire upper-respiratory system.

Or so it felt like.

By the time they popped him out of the chamber on the other side, Cayson was fresh and clean, dressed in snow-white pajamas. He felt oh so sleepy.

Leland and Dmitri were waiting for him. They stopped chatting when they saw him.

Leland waved. "This way, cuz."

Dmitri lifted his hand, palm out, and a door slid open.

The stroll down a hallway made Cayson's knees weak, as if he were heading toward a lethal injection. "Will it hurt?"

"You know the answer," Dmitri said.

The hallway narrowed toward an unnumbered door that opened on its own when the trio approached it.

Inside was another whole cave full of buzzing worker bees—

Bees? Huh?

"I'm losing my mind." Cayson stared at the

dozens of busy lab technicians and workers swarming the heart of Moscow Mechanics.

"Hang in there," Leland said. "It'll be over soon."

Cayson frowned. "The next time a new potential customer calls, remind me that it's not worth five million dollars."

"It's not worth any amount, cuz. The love of money is the root of all evil."

"You talked to Byron?" Cayson remembered the counseling session with Byron Moss from church shortly after Cayson had failed to kill himself.

For the love of money is a root of all kinds of evil, for which some have strayed from the faith in their greediness, and pierced themselves through with many sorrows.

"You know it's in the Bible. First Timothy somewhere. God had first dibs on wisdom." Leland looked up the verse on her tablet. "Here it is. 1 Timothy 6:10."

Cayson nodded. He felt determined that if he survived this, he'd read the Bible more. Sign up for every ministry opportunity at church. Walk on the straight and narrow path.

Propose to Stella as soon as possible.

His eyes widened. How did *that* thought get into his head?

In the center of the cybernetics laboratory, the two owners of Moscow Mechanics waited silently as the lab technicians ushered Cayson to a row of pods, where he assumed that Icarus would be linked to the main server conducting the raid on MedusaNet.

Passing by Dmitri and Raj, Cayson nodded, as if saying his farewell.

"Oh, don't look so grim, friend," Dmitri said. "It's not that bad."

Raj concurred. "It's not like you'd totally die."

"Totally die? As in, there's such a thing as partially dying?" Cayson blurted.

Dmitri patted him on the shoulder. "Leland will be with you."

"Leland? No. Keep my cousin out of this. She has to go home alive, not brain damaged."

Raj pointed to another pod. "She's already buckled in. Let's not keep her waiting."

"Why? What for?"

"She's going to tether to you. Buddy system and all that." Raj waved.

Was that money speaking?

"No," Cayson snapped. "It's too dangerous."

"Don't worry. I'm invested in this," Raj explained. "I don't want either of you to die. In fact, I still want to buy Binary Systems and have you work for me."

"Work *with* you, not *for* you," Leland shouted from her pod.

"There, my business partner has spoken." Cayson managed a nervous smile.

"We'll need to work on soundproofing the pods better," Raj said to his lab manager.

The woman made some notes on her tablet.

As Cayson was entering his pod, he saw the logo on the door.

DARPA.

"Have we come full circle?" he asked no one in particular.

The Defense Advanced Research Projects Agency had invented the prototype implants that preceded Icarus for the purpose of creating super-soldiers for the Department of Defense.

Unfortunately, it had fallen into enemy hands. And one of those modified implants had found its way into Cayson's head.

And back into the lap of DARPA, the original incubator of them all.

"Icarus, are you okay?" Cayson didn't know why he asked.

I'm not Okay. I'm Icarus.

"Never mind."

Cayson sat down and waited. He felt a tickle behind his ear when the Bluetooth connection came to life.

"No helmet for me?" Cayson joked.

The pretty technician with the super-straight teeth chuckled. "That's so last century."

She shut the door behind him, and he was alone in the dark in a super-cold pod and with a sudden need to go to the little boys' room.

Suddenly, a virtual screen appeared on the pod wall to the left of the workstation in front of Cayson.

"You okay?" It was Dmitri.

His comforting grandfatherly voice surprised Cayson. He had known Dmitri to be hands-on, but hadn't the senior Russian hacker retired from cybernetics and chasing after cyberterrorists?

Dmitri looked like he was in another pod similar to Cayson's. However, on Dmitri's table was a blob of green slime.

Why does it always have to be green?

"What's that?" Cayson asked.

"What was in Dr. Reyes's head," Dmitri replied.

"Another Icarus?"

"No. This one's called Archimedes."

Before Cayson could ask any more, another virtual screen on the other side of his workstation flickered to life.

Onscreen, Leland waved. "You ready, cuz?"

Before Cayson could reply, Leland spoke again. "Okay then. Let's go take down the gorgon."

CHAPTER TWENTY-FIVE

Forty-six or forty-seven hours later, Cayson had gotten used to his new environment, where Icarus was getting closer to leaving his head, hopping on a data transfer cable, and making his residence inside a DARPA workstation connected to Cayson's head in this sterile cybernetics lab.

It still baffled Cayson that the Defense Advanced Research Projects Agency had created Icarus.

The entire project had been so hush-hush that Cayson was not given the entire picture. He could protest, but at this point, he just wanted Icarus out of his head.

What did Dmitri know?

One thing was certain: Dmitri had called DARPA instead of NSA.

Another thing was certain: DARPA was very interested in shutting down MedusaNet.

Something could be going on between Moscow Mechanics and DARPA.

But Cayson wouldn't be privy to it.

Right now, a bigger problem hung over them like the sword of Damocles.

An entourage of DARPA cybernetics specialists and an array of Rhinotec hackers from Raj's security company were all still at it, tinkering on the virtual padlocks that wrapped around MedusaNet like a tightly fitting exoskeleton.

There was no way in.

There was no way out.

In the midst of it all, Cayson didn't want them to sacrifice Icarus to destroy MedusaNet. Surely there was some other way?

But Icarus was the key, the backdoor.

Archimedes, the other implant, had been damaged when Dr. Reyes's head had exploded in Dmitri's farmhouse.

Icarus was the only perfect specimen.

Cayson closed his eyes. "Icarus, are we best buds?"

Bud? As in organism? Plant?

"Never mind." Cayson wiped trickles of sweat off the base of his jawline. When he looked down at his palm, he realized it wasn't sweat.

"Dmitri?" His voice cracked.

Dmitri turned toward the camera on the virtual screen. "Yes?"

"I'm bleeding."

"What?" Leland gasped on the other screen.

Cayson felt a headache coming. He began to pray.

And thought of Stella and their kiss in the meadow in the middle of nowhere in North Georgia. Her dress fluttered in the September breeze.

Lord, don't let me die before I tell her what I need to tell her.

He heard a door open behind him. His chair rotated. Now he faced the door.

One of the DARPA specialists peeked in. "Let's have a look."

Cayson wanted to get out of his seat, but that wasn't why they opened the door. Before Cayson realized it, she had withdrawn the syringe from the base of his head.

"W-what was that?" Cayson asked.

"Painkiller. It won't help, but you'll think it does."

"W-what?" Cayson felt dizzy.

Then he felt faint.

The pod disappeared from his view.

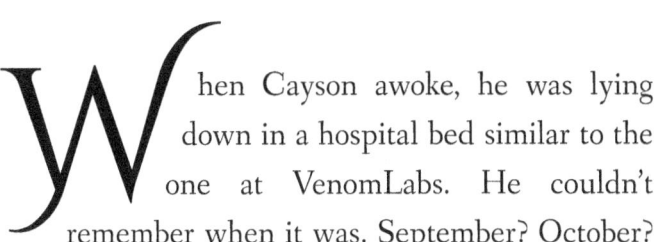

When Cayson awoke, he was lying down in a hospital bed similar to the one at VenomLabs. He couldn't remember when it was. September? October? It was all a blur, a veritable mash in his brain.

Icarus.

For a moment, he wondered if that had been his own thought or whether Icarus had just spoken to him, calling its own name.

He stared at the ceiling, afraid to move.

Instinctively, he reached up to touch behind his ear.

Nothing sticky. Instead, he felt a Band-Aid there.

Great.

"Icarus?" Cayson spoke louder now.

Or had he actually thought the word earlier rather than spoken it?

No reply from Icarus.

He felt alone with only the EKG and other machines around the hospital bed.

"Can I get some water, please?" he asked no one.

Water came on a tray, carried by a cybernetics lab technician, followed by familiar faces.

Dmitri, Leland, and Raj—whom Cayson hadn't talked to much.

"How are you feeling?" Leland limped toward her cousin.

"I should be asking you that." Cayson pointed to her leg, remembering the bombing at Venom-Labs back in September. "How's that foot?"

"Nothing a few stitches and painkillers can't handle."

"Yeah, you've always had a higher tolerance for pain than I do. You probably took after your father's side there. All the Yangs I know prefer our lives painless." Cayson returned the empty glass to the lab worker.

Leland looked alarmed. "Are the implants hurting your head?"

"You think?" Cayson chuckled. "Then again, it's not as bad as just now."

"Just now?" Dmitri knotted his eyebrows. "Just now when?"

"When my head was bleeding in the pod."

"That was four days ago, cuz," Leland said.

Four days?

"You were out for four days," Raj added. "We could not risk your death."

"Oh thank you, kind sir." Cayson closed his eyes. "Is Icarus still in my head? Why is it not responding?"

No one could answer him.

Dmitri patted his shoulder. "Why don't you rest? MedusaNet can wait."

They were all about to leave him, when Cayson asked for his cousin to stay.

Leland sat at the foot of his bed. "This looks comfy."

"When was the last time you slept?" Cayson asked.

Leland didn't reply.

"Sleep deprivation can kill you."

"I'll sleep when this is over," Leland said. "Let's try talking to Icarus again."

Cayson did. "He's not responding."

"Maybe he went to sleep." Leland laughed.

"Now that's a thought. Icarus, wake up."

Mole Rat.

Chameleon.

"That worked," Cayson said. "But I don't get what he's saying. He's repeating words he'd told me before."

"What words?" Leland was on her feet now.

"Mole Rat. Chameleon."

Leland called for her DARPA colleagues. She repeated the words.

"Decode it inside MAPL. Let's see what we find."

Cayson wondered about that interaction. After DARPA left, he asked Leland about it.

"Maple what?" he asked.

"M-A-P-L. I'll tell you later what it stands for, but it's an exaflop server—maybe even yottaflops, but they won't tell me."

"And you have access to it?"

Leland nodded.

"You ordering them around now?"

"I was going to tell you soon, cuz. While you were out for four days, I had to get us paid, you know?"

She had a head for business, just like Auntie Yang. Cayson had never been prouder. "And?"

"Like I said, you were out. So you can negotiate the terms later, if you don't like it."

"Terms? What terms?"

"I got us a contract with DARPA. I mean, we're here, right? So we need to be paid, obviously. Overtime and all that too."

"Right."

"Glad you gave me the majority share of the company?" Leland asked.

One percent.

That had been all it had taken for Cayson to lose control.

Then again...

He nodded. "You're the reason Binary Systems hasn't declared bankruptcy. You're good."

"No, cuz. God is good. His mercy is upon us."

"We might survive this yet."

The doors opened again, and DARPA was back.

Leland turned to Cayson and mouthed *yottaflops.*

The DARPA lady—Cayson reminded himself to ask for her name later—said something that Cayson hadn't expected at all.

"Mole Rat and Chameleon mapped to the original functions we created in DARPA for the prototype."

"The prototype with no name?" Cayson asked.

"It has a name, but we can't tell you."

"Will we find out later?"

"Irrelevant," she said.

Leland cut into their conversation. "What original functions?"

"Effectively, Icarus is the kill switch."

"For MedusaNet?" Leland asked.

The DARPA lady nodded.

Cayson stared straight ahead. "A kill switch in my head."

"Okay, we can do this," Leland concluded.

Cayson looked at his cousin. "If we're right, MedusaNet dies. But if we're wrong?"

"Then you die," Leland said.

CHAPTER TWENTY-SIX

For five weeks, they had hacked into MedusaNet. The virtual private network was dead, and Cayson was implant-free. He missed Icarus, but DARPA had promised to give him a sanitized personal version of it, whatever that meant.

Meanwhile, Cayson had another problem at Binary Systems.

Kelvin Gallagher had been missing since that September day they had attended the data storage conference in downtown Atlanta. The FBI and CIA were both looking for him, and so was the local police department.

He had vanished.

Leland continued to work with Raj Subramaniam, whose Rhinotec company was now seeking to buy VenomLabs.

Dmitri agreed to stay another week in Atlanta to help them hack into MedusaNet and shut it down. Well, that one week had extended to another four.

Altogether, it had taken ten weeks, ending in December.

By then, Stella had gone deep undercover, and Cayson had no idea where she was. Dmitri had promised to find out—in the spring.

Still, as far as Cayson's work at hand went, they had gotten it done, Dmitri and Leland—the professor and his protégé—together with Cayson, Raj, and a pack of hackers who didn't know what sleep was.

In the zero-sum scenario, the free world had earned one point and the terrorists zero. Whatever was lost by Molyneux was gained by free people everywhere.

After they did their work, Dmitri had a chat with Cayson and Leland.

Cayson couldn't believe it was nearly Christmas.

"The FSB wants to collect now," Dmitri said.

"So soon?" Another surprise for Cayson.

"I told you they would collect."

"But we just finished the project yesterday."

Dmitri nodded. "Cayson is still recovering from the de-implant surgery. Leland, start packing."

Cayson was about to protest, but Dmitri had more to say to Leland.

"The FSB will ensure your safety."

"How long is this project? What is this project?" Leland asked.

"You cannot ask me those questions. You will find out when you reach Moscow."

"You're going to leave me with strangers," Leland said.

Cayson stepped forward. "Like I said, I will go with you."

Dmitri looked at Leland, as if waiting for her to decide.

"Your scars." Leland pointed to the side of Cayson's head.

"Will always be there." With his thumb, he wiped a tear from Leland's cheek.

"I hate to break up this tender family moment, but no, Cayson, you can't go with Leland," Dmitri said.

"Why not?" Cayson asked.

"Because you and I are going to look for Kelvin Gallagher. Remember him?" Dmitri laughed. "I only have a few weeks to spare. Once we have a lead, we'll turn it over to Dario at the CIA."

Kelvin. Kel. Old buddy.

"And you know where to find him?" Cayson asked.

"The MOSSAD knows."

"MOSSAD? What has he done now?" Cayson rolled his eyes. Then he turned to Leland. "I don't want you to go alone though."

"Dario can go with me," Leland said.

Dario de la Cruz had always protected Leland, to the point that it made Cayson worry. What personal plans did the CIA agent have for Leland? Cayson could not begin to imagine.

"Moscow knows who she is. They like her. They want her," Dmitri said.

"That doesn't sound good." Cayson widened his eyes.

"Not to worry." Dmitri waved his arms. "They only want to borrow her hacking skills."

"And what might that be for?"

"They didn't say," Dmitri replied.

Leland patted Cayson's arm. "Don't worry about me. They gave their word to Dmitri, right?"

Dmitri nodded. "If it makes you feel better, I'll go with Leland for the first week."

"How long is this project again?" Leland asked.

"From a few weeks to a few months."

"Wait a minute. I'm going to miss Christmas with my parents?" Leland frowned. "Can we delay this until the first of the year?"

"You agreed. Now the payment is due," Dmitri said. "Our enemies are not taking holidays."

Leland sighed. "So the payment is due. Let's get it over and done with."

Cayson opened his mouth to say something when he felt a tap on his shoulder. He turned around to find Raj wishing them a good morning.

"Your tickets are booked," Raj said. "However, before you all leave, I need to borrow Cayson and Leland for a fifteen-minute meeting about the future of Binary Systems."

"Right now?" Cayson asked.

"Is there a better time than now?"

CHAPTER TWENTY-SEVEN

"I've sent my poor cousin to the wolves!"

It would have bothered Cayson more had Dmitri and Raj not kept him busy with the sudden three-million-dollar new assignment that had resulted from the dismantling of MedusaNet.

That VPN had proven that cyberterrorists had been smarter than VenomLabs, the NSA, the FBI, the CIA, and all other triple-letter entities now scrambling to clean up previously unknown security breaches.

Ironically, all that panic spelled more work for Binary Systems.

This new project involved building a security system around Moscow Mechanics.

"An impenetrable one," Raj, the half-owner of Moscow Mechanics, had said only the day before.

"Impossible," Cayson and Dmitri had replied in unison.

"Twenty million dollars says it can be done," the billionaire businessman from Bangalore had insisted.

That was the moment when Cayson had discovered that Binary Systems was paid a third of the cost of the entire project. Cayson thought it wasn't too bad.

Still, he wondered if they could have negotiated for more.

However, Raj had seemed to be more stubborn than Cayson had thought.

And he was still stubborn now, a week into this project.

Raj Subramaniam remained by Cayson's side, unmoving and unyielding to Cayson's request for room to breathe.

"Are you babysitting me?" Cayson asked.

"I'm babysitting my money." Raj's eyes didn't leave Cayson's, as if he were waiting for the latter to blink first.

Or waiting to see if Cayson had any visible side effects.

Cayson closed his eyes.

He couldn't feel Icarus anymore.

Once upon a time, he had felt something foreign in his head—like crawling roaches.

Now they were all dead.

In his head was radio silence.

DARPA, working with VenomLabs, had successfully removed Icarus from Cayson's head. Now it was upstairs in the cybernetics laboratory, being systematically reverse engineered.

And replicated.

Raj, Dmitri, and their DARPA and NSA counterparts were determined to reclaim Icarus and the next generation bots it could spawn.

Cayson wasn't sure what to think of that, though no one had asked for his opinion. If they had, he would have been ambivalent about what to do with Icarus.

Should they have destroyed Icarus? If they had, Molyneux's successor would only spawn new implants. Icarus would then become the prototype that bit the dust. Nobody would care.

Who was Cayson, a common hacker, to question the master hacker himself?

Dmitri should know what he was doing.

Cayson felt better. At least a little bit.

After all, Dmitri had always kept Cayson's best interests in mind. He had made another decision that made Cayson feel a little better. Dmitri had accompanied Leland to Moscow himself for the first week, helped her finish her project, and then brought her home.

Unfortunately, no sooner had Leland arrived in Atlanta, than Dario at the CIA had needed her help.

Bottomline: he could trust Dmitri, but not the FSB team that Leland had been sent to join. Code-named Wolves, they had sometimes played on both sides of the fence.

Had they really been with the FBI and INTERPOL against the terrorist Molyneux? Did anyone know for sure?

Just because they had helped INTERPOL apprehend Molyneux, didn't mean they were best buddies with the FBI now.

Friends for now didn't always translate into friends for life.

So.

The Wolves.

Yikes. Indeed, I've thrown my cousin to the wolves!

Cayson felt a nudge on his shoulder. Then a light pinch.

"Wake up!"

Raj's voice cut through Cayson's mental fog and rattled his brain.

Pinch, pinch.

"Owww!" Cayson rubbed his arm. "Did you just pinch me?"

He turned and found himself staring at a robot arm.

Raj retracted the arm, its fingers still in the act of pinching the air.

"On a scale of zero to ten, how much did you feel the pinches?" Raj asked.

"Pinches?" Cayson checked the red spots on his arm. "I want an addendum to my contract. Thou shalt not set any of your cyborg or robot body parts on me or any of my employees."

"Ask your lawyer to talk to my lawyer," Raj said.

"Fine."

"Good. That will keep you busy for a few weeks."

"What?"

"A few weeks of legal wrangling will take your mind off Leland." Raj smiled. "She's smart. Special. She should come work for me."

"Or you could pay Binary Systems for her to subcontract for you."

Raj chuckled. "Maybe you should pay me instead."

"Why?"

"Because Leland is fine, and that's what you want."

"Fine? Of course she's fine." Cayson prayed silently. "Dmitri was with her, and now Dario is."

"And my people." Raj put the robot arm on a nearby cart.

"Your people?" All sorts of possibilities lined up in Cayson's mind.

"My security team."

"Like what kind of security team?" Cayson was curious on the off chance that Raj's security team might include—

Nah. Stella was probably far away from Moscow.

"Shadows." And that seemed to be all Raj wanted to tell Cayson. "You can thank me later when she comes home safely."

"Thank you for caring."

"You and Leland are the core of Binary Systems. If I can't hire Leland directly, how about I buy your company? Name your price. And Kelvin can stay—if he doesn't end up serving time."

Cayson only focused on the last part of what Raj had said.

Kelvin could serve time.

Why?

Has he committed a crime?

What crime?

"What do you know about Kelvin?" Cayson asked.

"I know all about everyone who has ever worked for Binary Systems or Yottaflops or that other company you tried to start back when you were in college. Not all good things, but nobody is perfect."

"What for? Why do you need to know about us?"

"Need? More like for contingency reasons. We have clearances you don't even realize exist."

"I don't like all this shadow play." Cayson waved his arms about. "Shadow government stuff."

"Stella misses you," Raj said.

Whoa. "Where did that come from?"

"I told you we have privileges."

"And you mentioned Stella because..." Cayson felt slightly uncomfortable. This man knew a lot about the people Cayson cared about. Or did he really know?

What if Raj had simply made up the information?

In a virtual world, how could Cayson know which was real news and which was fake news?

"Your well-being matters to me," Raj explained. "Healthy hackers mean healthy business."

"So that's the bottom line." Cayson stared at the floor.

"The only bottom line," Raj said quietly.

Too quietly.

EPILOGUE

Stella Evans could identify that Hermès eau de toilette anywhere, even though the last time she had smelled it was a few years ago in Project Pericarp, when she had worked in close proximity with Cayson Yang.

When Stella saw him again seven months ago, Cayson did not smell like Hermès. He smelled like a scared human instead.

Through the grapevine, Stella had found out that by December of last year, Cayson was pretty much back to normal, with Icarus removed from his head for good.

Now, she smelled him again.

However, at two thousand feet above sea level, it had to be a coincidence.

Besides, when they had been together—survived together—eight months ago in Georgia, Cayson had not worn any cologne or fragrance.

All he had splashed on himself was an overdose of fear and fright.

Ah, wherever he is, I wish him well.

Stella folded her arms as she remained seated on the bare rock overlooking a crowd of people lining up to take turns to walk out onto the granite ledge.

Trolltunga.

A troll's tongue.

She closed her eyes, remembering that day eight months ago when she had found Cayson Yang standing over there—at the end of the world—and looking down into the throat of darkness.

Never again.

Cayson and his hackers at Binary Systems were safe now once they shut down MedusaNet, effectively killing the central command for the drones that had been programmed to track down Cayson via the homing beacon.

However, Vivek Rao and Danika Svoboda were still missing.

The eau de toilette lingered in Stella's nose. Funny how it was mixed with the smell of sweat.

Had it been eight months?

I miss him.

The noonday air was cool up in these mountains. March had dragged into April all around Stella as diminishing patches of snow still clung to the ground.

She'd have to hike down soon if she wanted to make it to the rental vehicle she had parked in the village of Skjeggedal before nightfall.

Then she would have to drive to Tyssedal, where her former colleagues had paid for her hotel as a farewell gift.

Farewell.

Saying farewell to her colleagues was one thing, but how could she ever say farewell to Cayson?

She closed her eyes and willed away a tear.

When she opened her eyes again, she couldn't believe who was sitting next to her. They were inches apart.

"You again." It was funny how her mind and mouth battled each other.

Her mind said, *I miss you.*

Her mouth said, "I quit. I'm retired."

"No, you're not retired. You're too young." Cayson Yang stretched his legs.

"I'm in my thirties."

"So am I. I'm older than you by nine-and-a-half months, and I'm still working."

Stella stared at him for the longest time. "You do look great. No more headaches?"

"None."

"How's Icarus?"

Cayson lifted his left wrist. "Icarus, say hello."

"Hello." The synthetic voice out of the watch had no emotion.

"I guess he's out of your head." Stella laughed. "Did you hike up all the way or take a chopper?"

Cayson frowned. "What? You think I'm not fit enough to hike up this mountain?"

"You don't look exhausted. I was."

"Well, I took frequent breaks."

"And still made it up here at noon."

Cayson shrugged. "I had a mission."

A mission. So had she the day she and Kessler had rescued Cayson from himself.

Back in September.

That seemed so long ago only because the last few months of work had been intense for her team.

Stella could not tell anyone outside the NCIJTF about what she and Jake Kessler had been doing between November and March. Well, there hadn't been much to tell except that they had rounded up all the other lesser moles except one.

They had failed to extract the Chamblee Mole embedded deep within the FBI.

In the process, Jake had been injured and his cover blown. Someone else had taken over the investigation.

New team, new members.

Stella could only pray that the new team had integrity and wouldn't turn out to be corrupted or in collusion with the Chamblee Mole.

Ah, another problem for another day.

After Jake Kessler had taken a sick leave, Stella had handed in her resignation, and returned to Atlanta to find Cayson Yang unavailable. He was working with Raj at VenomLabs, while Dmitri and Leland had gone overseas to hunt for Kelvin Gallagher, the missing system administrator—after the FBI had given up on the cold trail.

Then a month ago, Stella had received a cryptic call from Dmitri. He had news about the Chamblee Mole.

It seemed that Dmitri had information on just about anything and everything that Stella had been involved in.

How on earth had Dmitri known about the code name?

Still, a lead is a lead is a lead.

It had turned out that, with Mirabella by his side, Dmitri had returned to work at what used to be Moscow Mechanics. Dmitri and his business partner, Raj Subramaniam, had bought VenomLabs and merged all their cybernetics operations together in a new laboratory complex in metro Atlanta.

Somehow, in the course of overhauling their security systems, they had come across incriminating evidence related to the FBI mole.

Within weeks, Stella and Kessler had tracked down and captured the Chamblee Mole, a low-level new agent, clueless about what it meant to be an American citizen, and swearing allegiance to the wrong country.

Whatever.

It was no longer Stella's problem.

Her new problem, as things turned out, was sitting right here next to her.

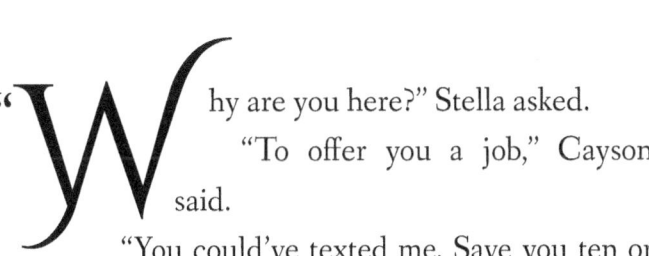

"Why are you here?" Stella asked.

"To offer you a job," Cayson said.

"You could've texted me. Save you ten or eleven hours."

Cayson ignored her retort. "Don't you know that you shouldn't be hiking alone?"

"Alone is what I need to be right now."

"Oh."

Silence passed between them through the nippy April air. It was partially cloudy, and Stella could not see the rest of the mountain ranges.

"Come work with me?" Cayson asked.

With me.

Not for me.

"Doing what?" Stella asked.

"Security."

"I'm done with that type of thing." Stella smiled. "I'm going to take up something benign, like gardening."

Truly, Stella didn't know why she had said that. Working with Cayson could have its perks.

And downfalls.

It would be awkward if they went out—

What am I saying?

"I've had a lot of time to think about my career, and maybe I don't need all that stress."

"Is that why you quit the bureau?"

Stella had her reasons, but she wasn't ready to share.

"I'm creating a security department at Binary Systems," Cayson said.

Stella almost told him to stop, but then something popped into her head. "You decided not to sell to Raj?"

"And be his VP? No. I prefer to be my own boss. Leland agrees with me, and so that's the way it goes. We'll subcontract for Raj."

Stella nodded. "Makes sense."

"The good news is that VenomLabs has outsourced their computer security to my company. We're getting super busy."

"Good for you and your cousin."

"Leland and Dmitri, together with our worldwide contacts, are still out there, looking for Kelvin. I've got other employees at Binary Systems who will work with me until she's available."

"How many employees do you have now?" Actually, Stella had wanted to word her question another way, but then it would be too much for Cayson to bear. *How many employees do you have left?*

"We lost three, as you know, and I will need to hire some new people." Cayson's voice was low, as if he had gone over this in his mind many times. "Kelvin and Leland are out of commission. I have five or six subcontractors I'm trying to turn into full-time salaried employees."

"More benefits for them."

"They don't see it that way. They value their

freedom more than healthcare," Cayson explained. "I wish Leland was back last month, to be honest. I can't do this without her."

"I'm assuming you consider Leland to be a better hacker than you are."

"No comparison. I think Raj is offering her a job, which I doubt she'll take—but then again, I don't always know what my cousin is thinking."

"Ah, so owning your own business runs in the family."

"I think we Yangs don't like to be told what to do." Cayson shrugged. "Or be forced to do what we don't want to do, like having implants in our heads —you know, against our will."

"I hear you." Stella shifted on the rock. "Any word on Kelvin?"

"No. There's nothing more we can do beyond looking, looking, looking."

"Associates? What sort of associates?" Stella looked around, wondering if—no, assuming—that someone was listening.

Tired hikers milled about on the top of the world. They clearly didn't care one way or another that Kelvin Gallagher was still missing. The world spun on even if Kelvin was in mortal danger.

"Everyone. He has friends who would help us."

"And enemies who would do us harm."

Cayson stared at her. "You never switch off work, do you?"

Stella wasn't sure how to answer that. While she had only been in the NCIJTF for a couple of years, it had been intense every week for that length of time. Like an over-the-top battle for survival.

Only deadlier.

"We're all stumped," Cayson added. "Raj is making it into a case study. How do you track someone who has vanished?"

"You know the answer. We never totally vanish in this day and age."

"Ah, therein is the paradox." Cayson smiled. "Unfortunately, even the best hackers in the world can't find him."

"You're assuming that Binary Systems has the best hackers in the world."

"I'm saying exactly that."

Stella didn't respond to that stroke of pride. Or arrogance.

Stella wondered where Leland was now. She was probably not in Moscow.

Ah, a story for another day.

"So how about my job offer?" Cayson asked again, as if his question required an answer.

"When do you need to know?"

"Soon, I hope." Cayson smiled. "Maybe I can persuade you."

"How?"

"By spending more time with you."

"That would be counterproductive." Stella leaned away. "Besides, what would we be doing together?"

"I don't know. Coffee. A walk in the park. Whatever you want."

Coffee? That's harmless.

"A walk in the park? That doesn't sound like business."

"Business?" Cayson seemed taken aback. "Oh yes, the job at my company."

"Lost your train of thought?"

"I was just remembering last year..."

Me too.

"I meant it."

I know you did.

Cayson stood up and pulled Stella to her feet. "Well, we have five or six hours of daylight left. The first order of business is to hike down this mountain."

Stella brushed off bits of dirt and wet grass from her pants.

"Then coffee?" Cayson lifted his eyebrows.

"We can start with coffee and go from there,"

Stella said quietly.

"To lunch, maybe?"

"Or dinner, depending."

"I'd like that." He reached for Stella's hand.

She didn't pull away.

"Marry me?" Cayson suddenly said.

Two words. He seemed to have made it simple for himself.

Stella wondered how many times he'd practiced that. "Where did that come from?"

"My heart." Cayson knelt down. "But you could've guessed. Since that day in the open field..."

In the forests around Dahlonega...

Stella had thought about it too. And prayed about it for months since they had gone their separate ways after Atlanta. She knew what she would say if he ever popped the question.

Then again, could it be too soon?

Her heart wanted to say *yes* to being with Cayson for the rest of her life.

Her head said they should wait a bit.

Stella pulled him to his feet and wrapped her arms around his waist. "I need time to process this."

"This?"

"Our future together."

Cayson looked disappointed.

"Ask me again?" Stella whispered.

"Just so you know, I've prayed about it."

"So have I." Stella kissed the edge of Cayson's lips. "We will know when we both have God's peace about it."

Which I do now, but...

Just have to be sure.

Cayson nodded, as if understanding.

They stood there, hugging, nothing more to say until Cayson broke their silence. "But now, coffee."

"Of course. Let's go get coffee."

And they held hands all the way down the mountain.

At the bottom of the mountain, Cayson asked her again.

And Stella said, "Yes."

Dear Reader:

Thank you for reading *Zero Sum*, Book 1 in the Binary Hackers series, a mix of futuristic technology and science fiction set in the near future, in which I explore what would happen if humans twist this concept or turn that truth.

The next book is stray hacker Kelvin Gallagher's story. *Zero Day* takes us behind the scene to the other side, to the people who enabled terrorists to make the cybernetic implants for a nefarious purpose and to the moral battles in their minds.

I started writing Kelvin's story when I pondered what would happen to a hacker who straddles the fence between wanting to do what is right while doing all the wrong things.

We met Kelvin in the first pages of *Zero Sum*, shortly before he is whisked away to parts unknown. In *Zero Day*, we pick up his story some months afterwards, when he finds himself in a rat-infested abandoned building in Prague, waiting to die.

Zero Day (Binary Hackers Book 2)
JanThompson.com/zeroday

Meet the Supporting Cast

In *Zero Sum*, we meet several people who have appeared before or will appear again in some of my other collections. Here are a few notable ones.

Byron Moss is in SMILE FOR ME

On a spiritual level, Cayson finds comfort praying to God and seeking His Word, even as he suffers through the ordeal. I remind myself that in our times of hardship, God brings other Christians to comfort us. In *Zero Sum*, Cayson's cousin Leland, counseling pastor Byron Moss from the Vacation Sweethearts series, and his love interest, Stella, all offer him support and encouragement.

Smile for Me (Vacation Sweethearts Book 1)
JanThompson.com/smile

Leland Yang-Joule travels across my story world...

Cayson Yang's cousin, Leland Yang-Joule, is the other co-founder of Binary Systems, Inc. Leland first appears on the scene when she is summoned to help recover treasures from World War II in Helen Hu's story, *Once a Thief* (Protector Sweethearts Book 1). Leland will appear again in the next book in the Binary Hackers series, and also in a future romantic thriller series of her own.

Once a Thief (Protector Sweethearts Book 1)

JanThompson.com/oncethief

Zero Day (Binary Hackers Book 2)
JanThompson.com/zeroday

Jake Kessler is in ONCE A HERO

Jake Kessler goes undercover in *Reach for Me* (Vacation Sweethearts Book 2), where the hunt for Molyneux begins for him. Without going into spoilers, let's just say that Jake's cameo appearance in that novel sets the tone for *Once a Hero* (Protector Sweethearts Book 2), where Jake gets his own story.

Reach for Me (Vacation Sweethearts Book 2)
JanThompson.com/reach

Once a Hero (Protector Sweethearts Book 2)
JanThompson.com/oncehero

Sign up for my mailing list!

If you like Christian romantic suspense, near-future technothrillers, coastal and beach romance, and romantic women's fiction, feel free to sign up for my mailing list. I'm writing more books for you to enjoy.

JanThompson.com/newsletter

Would you please post a review?

I hope you enjoyed the story of Cayson and Stella. If you did, would you write a review of the book? Reviews are very helpful to other readers. Please follow the link below to post your review on a retailer site. Thank you very much!

Zero Sum (Binary Hackers Book 1)
JanThompson.com/zerosum

Sneak peek...

Continue reading for a chapter preview of *Zero Day*.

THE NEXT BOOK IS ZERO DAY
BINARY HACKERS BOOK 2

A maligned hacker.
A Mossad agent.
A mutual enemy.

No longer of any use to the governments who once coveted his cybercriminal mind, disgraced hacker

Kelvin Gallagher finds himself languishing in Prague while waiting for his enemies to find him and end his sufferings. Along comes a Mossad agent, once a friend, but now determined to take him home in a body bag...

Zero Day is book 2 in my **Binary Hackers** series of inspirational near-future cyberthrillers combining technothriller and romance. If you're looking for clean suspense without compromising faith, these books might be for you.

The prisoner awaits...

Down and out and waiting to die, mercenary hacker Kelvin Gallagher regrets betraying his homeland. Rejected by everyone, Kelvin has no choice but dig deeper into the dark hole into which he has fallen.

He remembers his ex-employers at Binary Systems Inc., who have given him a job when nobody else dared. Are Cayson Yang and Leland Yang-Joule more moral than he is? He thinks not. Aren't they all working for money?

Yeah, life is worth more than money. Kelvin knows that, but it's too late. Way too late as he sits in a rat-infested rundown building in Old Prague, fearful and in anguish.

The executioner comes...

As an act of revenge, former Mossad agent Yona Epstein tracks down the American traitor who led her mentor to the slaughterhouse. It makes Yona angry that Kelvin used to be a friend, back when they worked together in a project.

When Yona uncovers Kelvin's hideout in Europe, she realizes she isn't the only one who wants Kelvin dead. That makes her pause.

To kill or not to kill...

When Kelvin explains to Yona his version of the cybercrime nightmare of his own making, several events don't match up with what Yona has been told by her associates.

Is Kelvin innocent after all? Should Yona delay the execution until she finds out what is going on? Or proceed based on the information she already has? She trusts her sources, doesn't she?

～

Zero Day (Binary Hackers Book 2)
JanThompson.com/zeroday

Binary Hackers
JanThompson.com/binary

Book News from Jan Thompson:
JanThompson.com/newsletter

ZERO DAY CHAPTER 1
SNEAK PEEK
BINARY HACKERS BOOK 2

Tuna and shrimp for dinner tonight wouldn't have smelled this bad to Kelvin Gallagher if it hadn't been from a can he shared with Mordecai the stray cat who came to his fourth floor hideout every couple of nights to kill rats for him.

This hadn't been how Kelvin envisioned his last days on earth, sitting on death row in a condemned building in Old Town Prague, waiting for God to take him to Heaven where he expected to feast at the table with the King of Kings and Lord of Lords.

Meanwhile, cat food.

Kelvin gagged.

He pushed the can away, and as if on cue, His

Royal Catness appeared through the crack in the broken wooden slats in the window, trotting toward the heavenly smell.

"Have it all." Again. "Don't worry about me. I need to lose weight, anyway."

It was dusk outside. It felt like dusk. But he dared not peek out of the window, as if doing so would hasten his own demise.

Someone would see him.

The elderly grandmother two doors down was the only person who knew he was hiding in this building, only because she had fed him dried pork and leftover pickled vegetables every now and then. And because she allowed him to take a quick shower in her house once a week to conserve water.

Tereza's heart of gold could get her killed.

I must leave. But where do I go?

No passport. No work visa. No money.

He was now an illegal alien in the Czech Republic, dumped here by rogue Federal Security Service of the Russian Federation agents who had wrestled him out of Aspasia's hands. They had no use for him any more since MedusaNet was all but shut down. So they dropped him off in Prague to protect themselves from liability.

Yeah, liability.

Those former FSB agents were more like

mercenaries, thinking they would earn a whole lot more American dollars freelancing than if they had worked as salaried employees of the Russian government.

Ironically, they hadn't left him here in the pursuit of money. They had left him here for assassins to find him—if Aspasia didn't find him first.

Kelvin berated himself repeatedly for not asking those people for at least a fake passport and some koruny české or maybe even euro banknotes.

"I'm all alone. I have to get out of this myself." Kelvin wrapped his arms around his bended knees and leaned back against the wall, paint peeling off here and there. "Where are you, God? I need a miracle. I need a miracle."

Why didn't God stop him from leaving Atlanta eight months before? If he had remained in town, his employers at Binary Systems would have found them.

What choice did he have, honestly? There he was that fateful day in September, walking around the convention floor, snacking and picking up free merchandise, when out of the corner of his eye he spotted Aspasia walking toward the YottaFlops booth that he and his employer, Cayson Yang, had set up.

He wanted to warn Cayson, but he saw the

woman spray some sort of liquid in Cayson's face. Then he watched his boss go down just before she stabbed the side of his head with some sort of device.

Which he later found out to have activated the cybernetic implant in Cayson's head.

She looked up from the floor and stared straight at Kelvin.

Kelvin remembered dropping the 3D-printed bobblehead doll of himself, and running for his life. It didn't help that he had worn a bright yellow tee shirt.

Aspasia caught up with him in no time, with those FSB agents not too far behind her.

And here I am.

Well, yeah, by way of Moscow, but that was the part Kelvin didn't want to think about.

"Meow."

Looking past the cat, Kelvin saw the empty can on the old wooden floor.

"That's all I got, buddy." Kelvin shuffled his way to his makeshift bed at a corner of the room.

His bed was a pile of old, torn blankets he had salvaged from the neighborhood dumpsters. On top of it was a plastic bag he had stuffed with rags. He puffed it up and put his head on it.

Mordecai came over and sat on the blanket

with him. He cleaned his gray fur, speckled with white.

"When I leave this place, I'll take you with me, okay?" Kelvin tapped his head. The cat purred. "That is, if I physically leave. If I die, then I can't keep my word, you know."

The gray cat settled down at an edge of Kelvin's blanket and began to clean his paws.

Kelvin felt thirsty. He stared at the crack in the ceiling. He worried that the ceiling would cave in, though ironically it would usher in a faster death for him.

Was death the only way out?

He wasn't sure.

He tried to pray, but no words came to his mind or mouth. He had been a churchgoer back in Atlanta, in his younger carefree days when he wanted to do everything right in the eyes of God.

No eventuality like this ever crossed his mind.

No, his goal was to buy his mother a house on the beach on Tybee Island, provide her with a personal chef and housekeeper. She could spend her days reading books on the balcony overlooking the Atlantic Ocean.

That had been his goal.

Until her lung cancer worsened, and Kelvin needed money quickly before time ran out. She never went into remission, and three months after the chemotherapy, she asked to be taken off treatment so that she could die in peace at home.

That had been when Aspasia showed up, offering Kelvin a job behind the job. All he had to do was plant backdoors into their network they were constructing for Birmingham Bytes, a British company with international clients.

Kelvin dusted off his hacking skills and joined the covert team. It was a win-win. He could moonlight the project and still keep his day job as a system administrator at Binary Systems.

He would walk away with a cool ten million dollars.

Easy money.

Yeah.

The cat snuggled next to him, and Kelvin closed his eyes.

He saw his mother laughing and smiling, walking at the ocean's edge on Tybee Island against a backdrop of the five-million-dollar oceanfront home he had bought for her. He still had another five million to splurge on her.

He remembered how his mother kissed him on the forehead in their last days together, just as she had done all his life whenever he had been a good boy. Little did she know that he had sold his soul to buy her the mansion.

And two months later, she passed away.

The beachfront house, paid in cash through an overseas company, became vacant after Mother died. Kelvin didn't want to stay there.

Soon thereafter, Birmingham Bytes went out of business and its assets were sold to pay off their debts. Little did anyone know that MedusaNet would be sold to Molyneux, a terrorist at large who had stolen from everybody from MI-6 to the CIA and everyone in between.

The other shoe dropped when Kelvin learned that the network he had been hired to test and protect was none other than MedusaNet.

He had no choice but to do what Aspasia wanted. She threatened to kill his mother. Even though she was dying of cancer, Kelvin wanted to give her the best end-of-life care ever.

After Aspasia let him go home for his mother's funeral, he sold the beach house, breaking even, and tried to return the money to Aspasia. She wouldn't take it.

She simply wouldn't take it back.

If he had...

If only...

Nah.

Hindsight could not save him now. "I reaped what I sowed."

Be not deceived; God is not mocked: for whatsoever a man soweth, that shall he also reap.

Galatians 6:7 couldn't help him now. The deed had been done.

In fact, Aspasia had threatened him with death if he went to the authorities.

There was no way Kelvin could go to the police at all. He would end up implicating himself. That company, Birmingham Bytes, no longer existed. It had served its purpose, and now was absorbed into the MedusaNet systems.

Too late.

"Everything is too late." Kelvin sighed as rain fell on the roof.

He opened his eyes and jumped out of bed. He gathered up a few cups and a can, opened the window slightly and placed the chipped cups and dented cans on the window sill. Rainwater dripped into the cups.

"Thank you, God, for water." Kelvin stuck his head out, and washed his hair in the rain.

The night was dark and he could not see beyond the dim moonlight. He prayed that nobody saw his face out here.

Outside his windows were rows of tiled roofs—

red during the day—stretching all the way to the Vltava River, or at least the street in front of it.

The rain beat down noisily, and he could not hear the city tonight. The music festival had just started a day or two ago. Sometimes during the day, he could hear music and the crowd, though he could not see Charles Bridge from here, five blocks away.

There was music, festivities, food...

Kelvin's stomach rumbled. He reached out for one of the dirty cups. There was already half an inch of water in there. He poured it into another cup. And did so with the other cups until he had one cup of water.

"Diet dinner." He chuckled.

Zero Day (Binary Hackers Book 2)
JanThompson.com/zeroday

Binary Hackers
JanThompson.com/binary

Book News from Jan Thompson:
JanThompson.com/newsletter

ACKNOWLEDGMENTS

Many thanks to my Georgia Press publishing team for keeping up with my busy schedule for this book.

My copyeditor, Dori Harrell, is tireless and timely. My proofreaders, Lesley McDaniel and Lenda Selph, have sharp eyes from the Lord. Thank you, ladies!

Regarding FBI procedural information, I thank private investigator and former FBI agent Steven Kerry Brown for answering all my fact-checking questions. However, all invented processes and creative liberties are mine.

I also want to thank my husband and our son for their constant support and encouragement.

And I'll always remember my beloved mother and my late father for having instilled in me the love of reading and writing from a very early age. I miss my father here on earth, but I will see him in heaven some bright day.

Most of all, I am eternally thankful to my Lord and Savior, Jesus Christ, who died on the cross to save me from my sins and rose again from the grave to give me eternal life. Without Him, I can write nothing.

Jan Thompson
John 3:16

BOOKS BY JAN THOMPSON

Contemporary Christian City, Coastal, and Beach Romance

Seaside Chapel (7 Books)
JanThompson.com/seaside
Savannah Sweethearts (12 Books)
JanThompson.com/savannah
Vacation Sweethearts (8 Books)
JanThompson.com/vacation

Christian Romantic Suspense and Near-Future Technothrillers

Protector Sweethearts (6 Books)
JanThompson.com/protector
Defender Sweethearts (6 Books)
JanThompson.com/defender
Binary Hackers (4 Books)
JanThompson.com/binary

Subscribe to Jan Thompson's mailing list:
JanThompson.com/newsletter

BINARY HACKERS

Like more suspense with your Christian romance? Like to read suspense thrillers? If you're looking for clean near-future romantic suspense without compromising the Christian faith, these books are for you.

From *USA Today* bestselling author Jan Thompson come these inspirational near-future cyberthrillers combining technothriller and romance, starting with Binary Hackers that feature computer specialists living at the edge of cyberspace, where they have to juggle being law-abiding truth-telling Christians while carrying out their assignments by any and all means possible.

The Binary Hackers series is set in the same story world as Jan's other books, and characters from the other series may make cameo appearances in this series and vice versa.

- Book 1: *Zero Sum*
- Book 2: *Zero Day*
- Book 3: *Zero Base*
- Book 4: *Zero Trust*

For more information about Binary Hackers:
JanThompson.com/binary

PROTECTOR SWEETHEARTS

Private investigator Helen Hu and her associates specialize in searching for missing persons and hunting for lost treasures. Join them in their adventure suspense around the world in *USA Today* bestselling author Jan Thompson's Protector Sweethearts, a series of Christian Romantic Suspense with a side of mystery.

Protector Sweethearts is a spin-off of Savannah Sweethearts and Vacation Sweethearts.

- Book 1: *Once a Thief*
- Book 2: *Once a Hero*
- Book 3: *Once a Spy*
- Book 4: *Twice a Fighter*

- Book 5: *Twice a Convict*
- Book 6: *Twice a Soldier*

For more information about Protector Sweethearts:
JanThompson.com/protector

DEFENDER SWEETHEARTS

Defender Sweethearts is a sister series to the Protector Sweethearts Christian romantic suspense collection. While the heroes in Protector Sweethearts search for lost treasures and lost people, the Defender Sweethearts novels focus on protecting the helpless and hopeless. The main characters in Defender Sweethearts come from the supporting cast in Protector Sweethearts.

- Book 1: *Never a Traitor*
- Book 2: *Never a Hostage*
- Book 3: *Never a Fugitive*
- Book 4: *Always a Maverick*
- Book 5: *Always a Champion*
- Book 6: *Always a Guardian*

For more information about Defender Sweethearts:
JanThompson.com/defender

SAVANNAH SWEETHEARTS

Welcome to the new south! From *USA Today* bestselling author Jan Thompson come these clean and wholesome, sweet and inspirational Christian romances set on the romantic beaches of Tybee Island and in the coastal town of Savannah, Georgia. Meet a group of multiracial and multiethnic churchgoing Christians who love the Lord, work hard in their careers, and seek God's will for their love lives. Against a backdrop of ocean, sand, and sun, these inspirational romances showcase aspects of the human need for God and for one another. Have some tea, settle in a comfortable reading chair, and enjoy these sweet celebrations of faith, hope, and love in Jesus Christ.

- Book 1: *Ask You Later* (Artist Romance)
- Book 2: *Know You More* (Multiracial Romance)
- Book 3: *Tell You Soon* (Asian-American Romance with Suspense)
- Book 4: *Draw You Near* (International Romance)
- Book 5: *Cherish You So* (Wheelchair Billionaire Romance)
- Book 6: *Walk You There* (Old-Meets-New Tour Guide Romance)
- Book 7: *Love You Always* (Romance with Suspense)
- Book 8: *Kiss You Now* (Multiracial Romance)
- Book 9: *Find You Again* (Multiracial Romance)
- Book 10: *Wish You Joy* (Christmas-Themed Romance)
- Book 11: *Call You Home* (Deaf Chef Romance)
- Book 12: *Let You Go* (Asian-American Romance with Suspense)

For more information about Savannah Sweethearts:
JanThompson.com/savannah

VACATION SWEETHEARTS

Travel with our friends from Savannah, Georgia, to the coast and to the mountains. Cheer them on as they celebrate the immeasurable grace and undeserved mercy of God through Jesus Christ.

The Vacation Sweethearts novels are a spin-off of Jan's Savannah Sweethearts series, and fans will recognize familiar faces from Riverside Chapel, a church in the coastal city of Savannah, Georgia. In fact, we might even visit the beach town of Tybee Island from time to time to visit old friends and beloved families...

- Book o (Prequel): *Time for Me*
- Book 1: *Smile for Me* (International Romance)

- Book 2: *Reach for Me* (Romance with Suspense)
- Book 3: *Wait for Me* (Romance with Suspense)
- Book 4: *Look for Me* (Romance with Suspense)
- Book 5: *Pray for Me* (International Romance)
- Book 6: *Care for Me* (Small Mountain Town Romance)
- Book 7: *Cheer for Me* (International Romance)

Read *Time for Me* (Prequel) for free:
JanThompson.com/time-free

For more information about Vacation Sweethearts:
JanThompson.com/vacation

SEASIDE CHAPEL

Welcome to *USA Today* bestselling author Jan Thompson's Seaside Chapel Christian beach romance series. These novels are set on real-life St. Simon's Island, Georgia—a beach town where history is all around and the future is a moment away—and the neighboring fictitious Seaside Island, where the rich and famous live.

Savor the small-town atmosphere and the warm southern beaches of St. Simon's Island and the idyllic Golden Isles along the Atlantic Ocean. Enjoy the music of the orchestra and hymns of the church, and hang out with our Christian friends who attend Seaside Chapel, a little church by the sea known for its beach weddings and fair share of love and life.

As these Christians grow in their knowledge and understanding of God, they are tested in their spiritual maturity, their love lives, and their relationships with others. Share their heartaches and healing, and cheer them on as they celebrate faith, family, and friends.

- Book 0 (Prequel): *His Surprise Proposal*
- Book 1: *His Longing Heart*
- Book 2: *His Wake-Up Call*
- Book 3: *His Morning Kiss*
- Book 4: *His Quiet Serenade*
- Book 5: *His Waiting Love*
- Book 6: *His Beach Retreat*

For more information about Seaside Chapel:
JanThompson.com/seaside

ABOUT JAN THOMPSON

USA Today bestselling author Jan Thompson writes clean and wholesome contemporary Christian romance with elements of women's fiction, Christian romantic suspense with an air of mystery, and inspirational international thrillers with threads of sweet Christian romance. Jan's books are for readers who love inspiring stories of faith, hope, and love in Jesus Christ.

Raised on a tropical island in the eastern hemisphere, Jan now lives and writes in the western hemisphere. Her international background gives her a unique multicultural and multiracial perspective to her novels and books. The island has never left her, and she reminisces about beach life in her beach romance novels.

When Jan is not busy writing small-town stories, she writes big-city romantic suspense and international technothrillers, a nod to her previous career in computer science. She weaves technology with human interests, reflecting the current and future digital world. And romance. There's always romance.

Beyond the printed page, Jan is a wife, mother, family scribe, avid reader, occasional artist, erstwhile pianist, and chief of staff to the family cat.

Find out more about Jan Thompson:
JanThompson.com

Subscribe to Jan's book news mailing list:
JanThompson.com/newsletter

For God so loved the world,
that He gave His only begotten Son,
that whosoever believeth in Him
should not perish,
but have everlasting life.
—John 3:16